THIS
WORLD
IS NOT
YOURS

THIS WORLD IS NOT YOURS

KEMI ASHING-GIWA

NIGHTFIRE

TOR PUBLISHING GROUP
NEW YORK

THIS WORLD IS NOT YOURS

A Nightfire Book
Published by Tom Doherty Associates / Tor Publishing Group
120 Broadway
New York, NY 10271

www.torpublishinggroup.com

Nightfire™ is a trademark of Macmillan Publishing Group, LLC.

The Library of Congress Cataloging-in-Publication Data
is available upon request.

ISBN 978-1-250-90186-6 (trade paperback)
ISBN 978-1-250-90187-3 (ebook)

Our books may be purchased in bulk for promotional, educational, or business use. Please contact your local bookseller or the Macmillan Corporate and Premium Sales Department at 1-800-221-7945, extension 5442, or by email at MacmillanSpecialMarkets@macmillan.com.

First Edition: 2024

Printed in the United States of America

0 9 8 7 6 5 4 3 2 1

To you, the reader

THIS
WORLD
IS NOT
YOURS

036

In the far reaches of space, a verdant planet becomes a world. The world observes the life It has made and, perceiving the life to be very good, is pleased.

But a critical piece is missing. Life is so very precious, so very fragile. How best to protect it? Walls can be scaled and poisons can be purged. All it takes are the right tools. No, the world needs something else.

Something . . . more.

The world takes care of Its own.

BEFORE

S he has two hours.

That's how long the grunts gave her. After that, anything's fair game. They didn't say those words explicitly, but she's been in the security industry for a while now. She completed the same "information extraction" tutorials as the local station officers. She knows what the thin smiles and blank eyes meant.

She's not proud of every scattered fragment of her past, of the things she had to do on the only jobs she could score. But these are the hardest orders she's ever had to follow.

It takes about two minutes to pack. She's always refused to call the duffel she stowed under the marble tiling in the foyer a go bag, but that's what it is. She told herself, over and over, that the extra changes of clothes, the ration packs, the flashlights and guns and solar chargers were for *them*. But the shirts are two sizes too large for her girlfriend, and there's only enough food to last one woman for long. Amara doesn't know the first thing about gun safety, anyway.

Leaving takes an eternity.

She takes one last look at her world before she goes.

She has to.

There's the satin-bound stack on the living room bookshelf, stuffed with every mortifying love note she wrote Amara when they first started dating. There's the tiny flower

Amara plucked from the palace gardens, pressed under a stack of books and presented to Vinh (so fucking proudly) two weeks ago, sitting on the coffee table. Hidden behind the cheap print Vinh scrounged up savings for is the newly installed safe Amara thinks Vinh doesn't know about, with a little velvet box Amara also thinks is a secret. They've laughed and wept in every room, bathed in the light of countless stars. They built a life here, together.

And now she has to leave it. Leave *her*. Forever.

She's almost died twice. Those long, agonizing moments pale in comparison to this.

She sees two final texts from her girlfriend before she wipes her talkglass, snaps it in half, and lobs it down the trash chute: *What do you want for dinner? I'm thinking we can order in?* Closely followed by: *Let me know. Love you so much!! :)*

Amara will be fine. She'll even be better off, and someday she'll find someone who actually deserves her, as soon as she realizes she always could've done better. Hot tears blur the room. But it's okay.

Vinh steps out of their apartment for the last time, the engraved steel doors rolling shut behind her like a tombstone.

035

They've been planning this for months, almost since they got back together a year ago.

Amara leans out the window of the helicraft, pointing toward the land below with the hand that isn't currently holding Vinh's. The ground is so bright with foliage it burns the eye just to look at it. Amara has taken so much for granted over the course of her thirty (conscious) years, but one thing she'll always deeply appreciate is the smell of life—the rich scent of fertile soil and the fresh perfume of flowers and the odor of animal sweat. The air on her family's residences, scattered across hundreds of orbiters and ships and stations, and even on the capital planet, is painfully pristine. It smells like nothing. This planet, their new world, is so different from everything she's ever known.

Vinh's eyes go wide. Amara watches as her girlfriend's gaze slides past the verdant forest flying by underneath them, latching onto the undulating, semitransparent *thing* moving toward the trees. It oozes over the red grass in an unstoppable, shapeless, swallowing tide.

"What the hell is that?" Vinh whispers into the microphone tip of her headset. Her fingers grip Amara's tighter.

Amara laughs, the wind whipping her dense brown curls about her face. She knows it's the same giggle that made

Vinh turn around in that club forever ago to get her first good look.

"Come on, I've shown you every picture I took for the council reports," says Amara. "Actually, I was worried you'd be bored if I took you here."

"Bored?" Vinh lets out a broken chuckle, pulling on a lock of straight black hair—an old nervous tic Amara hasn't seen in years. "*Bored?* Sweetheart, I'm terrified. The Gray—everything about it seems wrong."

Vinh is never scared. She's almost literally fearless. Bravery is action in the face of terror, certainly, but Vinh doesn't even need the courage her fellow security officers do. She just acts without fear, without a shred of hesitation or self-doubt. It's what makes her the settlement's best protector and the enemy's worst foe. The rival outpost of Jacksonhaven hasn't attempted a raid since she took over the security force.

Amara theorizes Vinh's problem here is that you and your forces can fight off a couple hundred grunts trying to steal food or fabricators, *but* you could fire a thousand rounds from a plasma cannon into the squirming mass below, and all you'd have is a busted cannon. If the Gray comes for them, there'd be nothing Vinh could do. All her training, all her skills—everything she is and everything she's worked for would be for nothing.

Amara lays her other hand over Vinh's in gentle reassurance. "I know it looks monstrous from a certain angle, but see?" She gestures toward the land below with a wide sweep of her palm. "The trees are untouched. If not for this loud hunk of metal, you'd still be able to hear all the animals." She smiles, almost fondly, as she surveys the sap-slow flood. "This is just the planet's self-cleaning mechanism. We could swim around in it and come out better than we went in. You can even breathe the Gray. In fact, the only time I've ever seen it attack two species at once was when they were in the same taxonomic tribe."

Vinh's mouth contorts into a grimace. "So what's it cleaning this time?"

"An invasive fungus from one of the other continents. We think Jacksonhaven brought it over from one of their surveys. Idiots." Amara smirks. "One of these days the planet's just going to get rid of them, I swear."

"Hm." Vinh's eyes flick up to the nearest hollow. It's a low, conical rupture, much like a squat volcano. But the planet's guts aren't solely magma. Instead of lava and toxic gas, hollows spew out the Gray.

If Jesse were here, which he isn't, he'd probably point out that there are, in fact, a number of genuine volcanoes in the sector. Their number and semi-frequent activity are part of the reason why the land is so fertile. Over the last several thousand years, their eruptions have showered the region with volcanic "ash"—nutrient-rich rock, mineral, and glass particles.

"But you said it never kills animals?"

"If that were really impossible, I probably would've been out of a job this past year," Amara says. "As far as I know, it hasn't. There's a chance the Gray *could* be a threat someday, but as long as we're careful, the probability of that happening is basically zero."

The Gray works across limited areas between hollows, hunting down the intended target with a ruthlessness Amara has to respect. As New Belaforme's head biologist, her job is to ensure the settlement is never seen as a contaminant, never perceived as the invasive species they technically are. She's taken thousands of samples, spent every day since being pulled from her sleep-cradle on Landing Day studying the digestive proteins that make up the Gray. They're fascinating molecular machines, flawlessly designed to reduce their targets to nothingness. Every week, she submits a report to the Council on everything they need to do to ensure the people of New Belaforme live in nothing less than perfect harmony with the planet. It's hard work, but critical. She's proud of herself, of every step she's taken without her family's power and privilege paving the way for her.

"It's sort of beautiful," says Vinh, pulling Amara from her thoughts. Her voice sounds very far away.

Amara hums her agreement. She's always thought so. The Gray isn't really gray; it's opalescent. In direct sunlight, its surface glitters with every color on the visible electromagnetic spectrum.

A herd of ungulate-class, ectothermic creatures run through the Gray, kicking up scintillating globules with their six hooved limbs. The herd leader shakes her arrowlike head, fluffing her magnificent striped mane. She throws open her tripartite, shell-piercing beak to let out a trill, the sound cutting through the helicraft's hum. Both women flinch and laugh.

"I've only heard that call in field recordings," Amara says, awed.

One specimen tucks in his legs, sits beside one of the arms of Gray creeping toward the forest, and starts sipping the fluid as the sun warms his hide.

"I know this is our life now. I know that being here, on this world and with you, is the new normal, but . . . I'm going to remember this trip for the rest of my days," says Amara, warmth swelling in her chest. She loves Vinh so much it hurts.

Vinh says nothing. For a moment Amara thinks she hasn't heard. Or maybe she's just so absorbed by the Gray. Amara understands the feeling—

Vinh sits back. Her cheeks, a few shades lighter than true copper, glow with a faint blush. Her eyes meet Amara's. "Do you want to get married?"

BEFORE

In a richly appointed private chamber, Amara weeps into Vinh's shoulder.

"I'm not even a person to them," Amara sobs. Her shoulders shake under three layers of gold-threaded silk. "Just another pawn, just another vessel for their dynasty."

"I know," murmurs Vinh, carding her fingers through Amara's hair. Her braids flow freely across her back, a rare sight; normally they're pulled up into an intricate coiffure. "I know. I'm so sorry."

They've been hiding away on a remote family estate, a diamond-shaped orbital station circling a turquoise gas giant at the edge of the system. Five minutes ago, Amara's family formally ordered her to return to the capital planet, where she will wed the politically advantageous match selected for her. Vinh is expected to disappear somewhere along the short journey. If she does not, there will be dire consequences for them both.

"I wish they could love me," Amara whispers. "Or . . . I wish I could just escape them."

They both know she wouldn't, even if she could. Amara's family is a supermassive black hole, each member orbiting around it like a blazing star. Together they form a galaxy, but even the greatest of them are helpless in the face of the singularity's thrall.

Vinh can't change that. But she *can* comfort Amara. "It's okay. You have me."

Amara lifts her forehead from Vinh's collarbone. Her eyes meet Vinh's.

"Promise?" she asks. They both know it's not a request.

Vinh's onyx-black eyes reflect the starscape outside with cutting clarity. A thousand suns glimmer in unshed tears. She brings a hand up to Amara's jaw, her thumb dragging gently across the other woman's cheek. "I promise," she says.

They both know it's not really an answer.

034

Amara is bouncing off the walls.

Jesse watches his best friend flit around her lab, trying very hard not to laugh. The fact that she's swaddled in a complete set of clunky personal protective equipment does not make this any less funny. What's less hilarious is that they've spent the past five hours in the bio sector's containment chamber, situated in the middle of a windowless basement and surrounded by nothing but steel, glass, and glaringly white plastic.

"Do you want to help me start the next run?"

"Amara, buddy, it's 9:15."

"I know, but I'm almost a week ahead of schedule." She yanks open the primary freezer. "Why not just go all the way?"

"I'm not sure if you know this," he says, unable to completely smother the twinge of humor in his voice, "but you're your own boss. It's not like the Council really understands what we're doing on a day-to-day basis, anyway."

"They understand more than you think," Amara says, only *mildly* chiding. There's hope. "And if they don't understand, then that's on us. Maybe we should implement a new format for our reports."

Jesse sighs, feeling almost sorry for Amara's hapless staff.

It's not like he's any better. "As long as you don't mention that I'm the reason why."

"Maybe I will, maybe I won't," she sings. "Do you want to help me start the next run or not, *buddy?*"

"You said you'd only stay an hour or two late," Jesse says, gloved fingers drumming against the polished black laminate of a workstation. "I could be home by now, eating dinner, but no."

"You could've left at any time," Amara says absently.

But I was waiting for you, Jesse doesn't say. He scrounges up the last of his patience. "So could you."

Amara slips a fresh slide into a microscope. "Fine. I'll start tomorrow. But come look at this for a second."

With a huff, he pushes himself up from the lab bench, glides across the floor, and looks over her shoulder at what she's doing. It would be . . . foolish, to say the least, to actively train the Gray to target humans, even if just to confirm that it could. That's what computer simulations are for. But even without testing animal samples, there's no end to the experiments they could run on the Gray. The last suite of trials was meant to determine whether the speed at which the Gray breaks down living tissue varies across different plants and microorganisms. It doesn't. It takes things apart, methodically, at the exact same rate.

And that slow, inexorable process is exactly what he sees now, as he brings the smooth expanse of his faceplate to the eyepiece. There's a cross section of stem here, with teardrop-shaped vascular bundles. Amara's shown him so many plant slides by now, recognizing the basic components is second nature. Large round water-conducting xylem vessels, tiny sugar-transporting phloem cells. A perfectly normal slice of stem, except for one little thing. Woven through it all are filaments of Gray, flickering like the tongues of snakes. Testing, tasting, and, cell by cell, devouring. Jesse can't help that the word *savoring* keeps coming to mind. He's seen this process a hundred times before, but each instance hits him like the very first.

"It seems so . . . alive," he murmurs.

He can almost hear the face Amara makes. "You know it's not."

"Then why are *you* in charge of studying it?" He doesn't take his eyes off the slide.

"Because I study life, and it acts like a life-form—" She cuts herself off once she realizes he's just fucking with her.

Jesse drags himself away from the microscope, grinning as she rolls her eyes.

She's right. Yes, the Gray has a sort of metabolism and it grows—it breaks down the constituent building blocks of whatever threat it was sent out for, and generates more of itself from those building blocks. It adapts to its environment, specifically to contain and reach its targets, and responds to certain stimuli. Whether it evolves is a more complicated question, but probably not a very pressing one. The important thing is that the Gray is not alive, no more so than a virus or a machine. But it *seems* biotic, so the Council deemed it prudent to treat it as if it were, and assigned a biologist to head the team monitoring it.

That's it. It's perfectly fine with Jesse. He's not jealous he didn't get first dibs on the Gray. He's not a *child*. Anyway, he crosses his arms and arches a brow at Amara, patiently prompting her to explain what's so special about this particular slide.

She grins, leaning her hip against the workstation. "It's bluebottle."

He can't believe they haven't decided on a proper name yet. "The squash that took over the coast a few months back?"

"Yeah." Amara's eyes are bright with excitement.

Jesse glances back at the microscope. "Is this an archived Gray sample?"

"No. It's fresh." She clasps her hands together. "Do you know what this means? Newly generated Gray attacks old invasive species it handled twelve-and-a-half weeks ago. It has some sort of long-term data storage."

Jesse's heart is beating very hard, very fast. "It remembers?"

Amara snorts. "Fool me once. Stop anthropomorphizing sludge."

"You know, intelligence and humanity are two different things," Jesse points out.

"Whatever. I'm going to get the new sample batch back in storage, since you've decided to be such a spoilsport. Be right back." With that, she plucks up a plastic tray and heads toward the decontamination unit.

So then it's just Jesse and the Gray.

Alone.

One minute passes. Then two.

Then his helmet is off, and he's pressing his eyes against the cool metal of the microscope's ocular lens. The Gray has completely deconstructed the plant tissue, and now it recedes into itself, task achieved. Sated.

He's about to pull off a glove—adjusting the focus is a nightmare with them on—when Amara walks in on him. He doesn't get the helmet back on quite fast enough.

"What are you doing!" she's yelling. She starts waving around her arms, like a delusional flightless bird trying to propel itself into the air. "I cannot believe you just compromised that sample, to say nothing of potentially endangering yourself! I—"

And so it begins.

She cares so, so much. It's why she gets on everyone's

nerves, why she's having trouble (again) with her fiancée. But not him. Never him. He understands that her nitpicking and badgering is only a facet of her affection. She understands him too. Mostly. Enough. He's working on it, but all relationships require effort, don't they?

Jesse acquiesces, chuckling, and nods along to her tirade. Amara won't be ready to let it go for a while, he knows; she chews him out the whole way back, and he lets her pleasant not-quite-screeching blur into the background.

Oh, how he loves her. She is *adorable*.

Oh, how he wishes he could fit her whole head in his mouth.

033

The evening sky is bright and cloudless and speckled with a tasteful scattering of early stars. Dusk stains the atmosphere with hints of purple and crimson, the last remnants of a particularly spectacular sunset. Triple-reinforced walls and tile roofs gleam a pristine white, even under the sunset. Elegant mosaics line airy hallways, glittering with rolling patterns of teal and turquoise. Music, just a little too catchy to sound truly improvised, drifts through cleverly concealed speakers. And, of course, there's Vinh. They're on their honeymoon.

Like every building owned by the Primacy of Cristoffa, the meditation retreat center is located less than five kilometers from New Belaforme. The miniature village is just far enough to allow its visitors the illusion of "getting away," but not so far that they can't flee to the main settlement if something happens.

Amara hears her wife—her *wife*! The thought makes her giddy—root around in the liquor cabinet before joining her on the suite's balcony. She sweeps across the floor toward Amara with a smile, two champagne flutes in hand. She's resplendent in a length of sun-bright yellow satin, twisted about her shoulders and fastened with a copper chain.

"How are you not cold?" Amara asks, accepting a glass. The temperature plummets fast on this planet.

Vinh's smile widens as she sinks down on the bench beside her. "You know I run hot." She laughs. "But I suspect you're asking for yourself." She snaps thrice, and heat floods from hidden vents. "Want a jacket?"

"I'm fine. Thank you." Amara takes a sip of champagne, wishing for coffee instead. The beverage she once despised has begun to grow on her. She takes it painfully sweet and half cream, a fact for which Vinh and Jesse both tease her.

Amara goes statue-still as a tiny birdlike creature—they've barely started classifying the life-forms here, and she hasn't had her weekly meeting with the resident ornithologist yet—alights on the balustrade to preen its golden plumes. She watches as Vinh extends an arm. The creature cocks its shimmering head, as if in thought, before flitting away.

Amara lets out a breath. "I'm going to have to speak to the supervisor. It shouldn't have been able to get through the field," she says, forcing herself to relax. "And *you* probably shouldn't go around trying to touch the fauna—"

"All right, I don't need a speech," Vinh says shortly. She would've sounded blithe to anyone who didn't know her, to anyone who hadn't trained themselves to hear the tightness in her voice.

Amara bites her lip. They're having a good time. Why ruin it?

To protect Vinh. Lush planets don't always ensure bountiful lives for settlers. Oftentimes the local life-forms are less than welcoming.

"It could've been venomous," she warns. "We have to be careful, sweetie. We have no idea how dangerous—"

"*Sweetie?* You realize you only use pet names when you're being condescending, don't you?" Vinh's voice is light and joking now, but her expression tells another story. Her beautiful eyes glare through an inky tangle of hair.

Amara chews the inside of her cheek. They're not really snapping at each other about terms of endearment. They're about to fight because Vinh is careless and Amara can't help but care. She knows that this is an argument that's been simmering for weeks, if not months. This moment is only the stupid little thing that turns up the flame. Still, it's an argument worth having, even if Amara doubts she'll get anywhere with her wife.

Amara puts down her glass and clasps her hands over her knees. "I nag because I love you."

Vinh deflates slightly. "I know." She makes a strange noise in the back of her throat and crosses her arms. "But I'm not a child. The fields have been updated to allow non-threat animals in."

"As the head biologist, I should have been notified."

Vinh's left eyebrow twitches. She stands and strides over to the balcony. "As the chief of security, I was going to. *After* our honeymoon."

This reminds Amara of the first few months of their courtship—long stretches of love and laughter punctuated by sharp, bitter bouts of anger and resentment. Amara hated it—the wobbling pattern they fell into. For every step forward, they inevitably took two back.

"You're right." *About what?* Amara asks herself, but she's learned the hard way that she occasionally needs to meet Vinh halfway, even when she's obviously correct. "I need to work on trusting you to take care of yourself, but it's hard."

Sometimes, trusting Vinh at all is hard.

Safety and security. One temporary, the other long-term. Vinh left Amara without a word once. She could do it again.

They've talked about what happened—Vinh apologized and they made up—but they've barely discussed what it meant. What it did to them and what they have. Every time Amara brings it up Vinh finds some new way of changing the subject. Or otherwise distracts her.

That time was a small death, and Amara doesn't want to relive it either. But refusing to address the pain they caused each other only hurts her more. Perhaps Vinh doesn't know that. Or maybe she can tell how guilty Amara feels about fixating on something that happened years ago, and she's trying to spare them both. Or maybe she knows and just doesn't care. Amara has no idea what's worse. A part of her doesn't want to know the answer. All that matters, she tells herself, is that they are together. At least, for as long as Vinh will have her.

"I'm sorry," she whispers.

"You are . . . everything . . . to me," Vinh says slowly, deliberately. She leans over the balcony, planting her elbows on the beam. Her fingers flex. "You know that, right?"

It's the truth; it's a lie.

"Do you think I'd ever recklessly endanger either of us?" Vinh continues, turning halfway around. Her eyes cut deeper than a scalpel. "I'd never risk *this*."

There is so much left unsaid, but they'll have time to say it later. Amara strides over and drops her temple to Vinh's shoulder.

Vinh reaches over and takes Amara's hand in hers. "You're freezing." A smile that doesn't quite reach her eyes, Amara's so sure of it. "Let me warm you up?"

Amara swallows her answering laugh, afraid it would turn to tears.

Vinh wriggles under the covers with an enormous yawn, and then she's out like a light. Amara has always envied that ability—she'd bet money the number of sleepless nights Vinh's suffered could be counted on a single hand.

She reaches out, brushing a stray lock of hair from Vinh's forehead. Something protective and fragile writhes between her ribs. Amara would kill for Vinh in a heartbeat and die for her in the next. She retracts her hand, tucks it under herself as she traces Vinh's features with her eyes. The thought of losing what they have—again—makes it dangerously hard to breathe. She depends on Vinh. She can only hope that Vinh needs her, too.

To become a subject of Cristoffa, Amara gave up everything. She gave up her Great Ọ̀yọ́ citizenship. She forfeited her inheritance, more than enough wealth to seed a small colony of her own. She formally disowned her family, not that doing so mattered much. This world is more than a hundred light-years from the nearest Great Ọ̀yọ́ outpost; if she deigned to send a message, everyone back home would be long dead before it ever reached them. (The ones who aren't flitting about the stars in cryosleep themselves, anyway.) Vinh and Jesse are all she has, the only people in the galaxy who matter.

Maybe it's wrong for Amara to need them like this. People should be complete by themselves. A strong foundation is built from strong stone; if one pillar falls the rest should remain upright. But when Amara tries to picture a life without her wife, she sees—nothing. There's a saying she half-remembers about a bundle of sticks being unbreakable while a single twig will snap. Vinh is the string that ties them all together, and Amara always verges on breaking.

———

Amara doesn't remember drifting off. She just finds herself awake when she wasn't a moment ago, pulled into consciousness as Vinh slips out from under the comforter. She reaches over to the nightstand, talkglass already in hand. She moves too fast for Amara to catch the name scrolling by on the device.

Amara reaches for her sleepily. "Where are you going?" she mumbles.

"I have to take a call. Security stuff."

Amara props herself up on an elbow, adrenaline spiking. "What's going on?"

"Don't worry. It's nothing serious. These clowns just can't do anything by themselves." Vinh shrugs on a jacket. "Don't let me keep you up."

"Come back to bed." Amara gnaws at the inside of her cheek when Vinh slips on her shoes. "If it's noncritical, you can deal with it in the morning."

"I'm always on the clock, you know that. What happened to Miss Head Biologist, anyway?" Vinh laughs.

Amara doesn't find anything funny. She sits all the way up now, rubbing at her eyes. "Vinh."

"I'll be right back." Vinh brushes a kiss over Amara's forehead on her way out. "Go back to sleep."

Amara falls back onto her pillow.

Vinh doesn't return until sunrise, exactly six hours and seventeen minutes later. That's 22,260 seconds. Amara knows because she couldn't sleep. She crawled out of bed, grabbed her workglass and removed her automatic vacation response. She's nearly cleared her inbox by the time Vinh comes in, yawning.

"Good morning." She drops a peck on Amara's cheek. "I'm going back to bed, wake me up when you get breakfast."

Then she's tugging off her clothes and diving under the covers without another word.

"I love you?" asks Amara, but her wife is already asleep.

NOTE TO SELF

REASONS TO LICK ROCKS

There are many reasons to lick rocks.

First, taste receptors are useful tools for detecting the presence of halite (sodium chloride, AKA salt) and sylvite (potassium chloride, isometrically quite similar) in a sample. Some porous rocks and minerals will, notably, stick to the tongue, such as kaolinite and chrysocolla.

It's quite tricky to differentiate shales from siltstones with the naked eye. Clay-based rocks like shale will dissolve into a fine paste, whereas siltstone will be a tad gritty.

It is sometimes easier to examine texture and assorted minute features in wet rocks, and if you were to find yourself in the field with limited water supplies, saliva does just fine.

Do not lick rocks with a metallic luster, and *definitely* do not lick minerals that are bright red, orange, yellow, green, or blue. Oftentimes such rocks will contain poisonous elements like mercury or arsenic.

In most cases, a simple touch of the tip of one's tongue ought to suffice.

—J.

032

A lone man hikes through the woods, accompanied only by the chirping of not-quite-birds, the chittering of beetle-analogues, and the friendly rustle of kaleidoscopically patterned trees.

They're finally gone.

He loves his friends, to an extent that almost terrifies him, but he needs his space. The vacation was his idea, obviously, a necessary reprieve Vinh and then Amara were nudged toward over the course of two long weeks. He loves them, but they exhaust him, in the way that all people a little too tied up in one another do. It's a genuine miracle that *they* manage, because whatever they have dwarfs what he possesses with the pair. The man tries not to feel insulted. He really, really tries. He prefers time with them individually for a reason.

Hopefully, the honeymoon will calm them down. Maybe by the time they get back they'll finally stop shoving the fact that they're unreasonably obsessed with each other in his face—

The man reaches his destination.

He sweeps aside a brilliant, parasitic curtain of crimson vines, which smother half the frilly-flowered fruit trees in the area. A delicate balance, both species kept in check by a multitude of factors.

And there it is. A shimmering pool of Gray, the last vestiges of a semi-recent flood in the area. Unlike most outpourings, though, it hasn't receded. Off comes the man's shirt, peeled away like a second skin, closely followed by his boots. He strides through the foliage framing the pool, bright, waxy, fernlike things with massive feathery leaves. There's a long, pregnant pause as he stands at the very edge.

He shouldn't be doing this. They're not supposed to even poke the Gray without proper protection, let alone swim in it. He has so little, though, besides *them,* and he needs something for himself. Just this one little thing. It's perfectly safe, anyway. Amara ran all the tests and then some, and she's an even better scientist than a friend. Which is saying a lot. Most of the time.

The man steps in. It's cold, at first, but the matrix around his toes warms almost instantaneously. Nothing out of the blue; the Gray just happens to be freakishly sensitive to temperature, and matches the heat of whatever it's touching. By the time he's up to his knees in the pool, it's like hopping into a warm bath. He lets himself sink, the Gray swallowing him centimeter by centimeter. His head bubbles under. When he opens his eyes, the world outside is pearlescent, as if viewed from behind diaphanous cloth.

He's not really interested in sleeping with either of them in any way but literally, maybe. The proximity would be nice, though, but it's not as if he can ask. It's not as if he has time to rest, anyway. He has so much work to do, lifetimes worth of studies to run. If the geology team doesn't hate him already, they will. Like Amara, he expects nothing but the best from his people, and won't tolerate anything less as they tease apart this planet's secrets.

He'd be getting even more done if he didn't have to deal with fucking Jacksonhaven. Now there are restricted areas,

and delays, and permits, and all the other nonsense the na-
ïve part of him had hoped he'd left behind on his homeworld.
His own polity isn't helping, either. He considers himself a
patient, easygoing man, but stupid bureaucratic bullshit that
could easily be avoided if everyone paused their pissing con-
test for five seconds . . . They've shed so much of one another's blood already.

When will it end?

Being in the Gray is supposed to relax him, but all he feels
now is fury. His heart rate spikes. The world flashes cinnabar-
red, coal-black, and gold-yellow, a dizzying array of classic
warning colors that vanishes as quickly as it began. Along
with the display comes burning flickers of . . . emotion? His
own feelings, reflected back . . .

In the Gray. *From* the Gray?

No.

No, no, no.

The man tries to lurch upright, but the Gray won't allow
it, like any self-respecting dilatant fluid. He moves slowly,
gently, rising to his feet at the bottom of the pool. He turns
a full circle.

Nothing, just more opalescent Gray, dotted with a couple
amphibian-looking creatures similarly looking for a good
time.

Sleep deprivation. A trick of the light.

That's all.

He needs air, now. His lungs burn for it. There is, of course,
the obvious solution.

He closes his eyes and drags in a deep, wet breath. A
twitching tendril of Gray slides down his throat, exploring.
It almost tickles and, nonsensically, that's what makes him
flinch in fear. But Jesse is a controlled man, a confident man,
ruled by logic and not flimsy things like mere feelings. He

knows the Gray matrix possesses sufficient concentrations of carbon dioxide and oxygen, with just enough space between the molecules. He can breathe normally, if he wants it badly enough. And he does. He strangles his panic, keeping perfectly still, and then his lungs are filling with an enthusiastic torrent. He empties his mind as best he can. Soon, but not soon enough, it's impossible to tell where he ends and the Gray begins.

Jesse is too far away, too deep in the Gray, to hear the first gunshots.

031

When the happy couple returns, Jesse is waiting for them on the landing pad. The first thing Amara notices is that he's not smiling. The second is the warm breeze carrying the acrid chemical tang of fire suppressant and disinfectant.

Blood rushes in her ears like a waterfall, so loud and quick it hurts. "What went wrong?"

Everything went wrong.

Jacksonhaven learned Vinh was gone while the newlyweds were returning. The rival colony sent twenty helicrafts to steal as many gestation chambers as they could carry, and destroyed the rest. Jacksonhaven's forces have always outnumbered them by at least three to one. When Vinh was there that didn't matter. She's always been smarter, faster, and more ruthless, and she trains her soldiers to be the same. As it turns out, the odds matter quite a lot when she's gone.

The raiders blasted all the fabricators too. Jacksonhaven saw the opportunity to doom the competition, securing the planet for themselves and for the Faceless Chancellor of the Amerigo asteroid belt—and they took it.

"Why wasn't I notified immediately?" Vinh demands. "I spoke with the Council hours before."

About what? Amara desperately wants to ask, but she knows this isn't the time.

"You don't think we tried?" Jesse asks quietly. "They made sure to take out communications first."

As Vinh paces across the landing pad, scarred hands in enraged fists, Jesse tries to console them with the knowledge that they'll more than likely survive.

"We can make our own clothes," he insists. "We can grow and cook our own food. And if we're careful with the tools we *do* have, we won't succumb to the elements."

This is why the Primacy gave them livestock in the first place. For emergencies, in case the fabricators failed or a rival settlement destroyed them.

"So we'll make it," Amara says, nodding her head.

Vinh stares into the rainforest. The canopy is just visible beyond the walls, like an upward meniscus of water atop the rim of a cup about to spill. She's looking toward Jackson-haven. "But New Belaforme won't."

"What do you mean?" Amara demands. But she knows.

Despite sporadic mass discoveries, there really aren't that many habitable planets in the galaxy, statistically speaking, and there are barely enough resources to inhabit them. Settlements are long-term investments. You don't pour more money into a bad venture. You let it die.

New Belaforme is not a flagship colony. Unless they get inordinately lucky and a wormhole pops up somewhere really convenient, the next resupply-collection Judgment ships won't arrive for a hundred years. The AI onboard will measure how much it's giving them versus how much it's collecting for the Primacy. When their descendants send up whatever pittance a handful of settlers will have been able to coax from the planet and ask for new fabricators and gestation chambers . . . the AI will recommend the Primacy simply strike New Belaforme from all records. A cold calculus, but one they all knew of when they signed up.

"Oh." Amara looks at her wife, at her best friend. Neither will meet her eyes. "We're fucked."

030

All the horror stories Amara's parents told her during her childhood, spent safe and pampered and ignored in their palaces, come flooding back into her mind. They're the same tales everyone else heard when they were little. The settlers on Pizarro IX choked down poison when the Judgment ship told them they'd be left to die. When their stores went bad, the New Cortés colonists drank filtered urine, and then blood for want of water. All that was left of the village were dried-out human husks. The stories go on and on and on.

In theory, it's possible that some of the forsaken settlements are doing fine. Just because they're no longer sponsored doesn't mean the colonists and their future generations will be any less talented or hardworking. They could survive. But such a miracle could only happen on a kind planet, a gentle, welcoming one.

This world is as brutal and unforgiving as it is beautiful. Without the support of the Primacy, New Belaforme will crumble. Not in their lives—if they're very lucky—or even this century, but it *will* happen. No far-flung colony on record has ever made it past its first half millennium without several visits from Judgment ships, infrequent as those visits are. Their people will begin the slow descent into madness, into anarchy, into bloodshed. New Belaforme will barely scrape by as it is with their meager stores, and things *will* continue to go wrong in the future. Their starving, desperate descendants will probably kill each other before malnourishment or sickness does. And who will mourn them? By the time the recommendation for abandoning the colony reaches the Primacy, they'd all be long dead.

"So what now?" In the shadow of the settlement's auditorium, Vinh presses her forehead to her wife's.

Amara nearly collapses under the weight of the question. Hushed voices, ranging from panicked to enraged to despairing, rush over her as other settlers exit the building behind them. The people of New Belaforme took the news as well as expected. Jacksonhaven's attack had been even more vicious than they previously thought. Given the decades-long stretches between Judgment ship visits, burgeoning colonies tend to work together for the first hundred or so years at least, when the benefits of cooperation outweigh the gains of competition. But polities don't like to share for long, so they all knew there would be future conflict. Only one government can rule a planet in the end, after all. Even so, they'd never expected violence of this level so soon.

"I don't know," Amara whispers. Her fingers wrap around Vinh's wrists as her wife cups her face. "I don't see how we can come back from this."

Vinh's eyes flutter closed. Her mouth crumples. Amara recalls the public disappearance of a Great Ọ̀yọ́ chancellor who pushed for the founding of a colony that went silent a month after its Landing Day. There are few things more politically damning than sponsoring a failed settlement, but that's the closest such tragedy has ever gotten to her life, before now. Vinh, on the other hand . . . Centuries ago, Vạn

Xuân seeded her home system with ten starter colonies. Even though the settlements worked together as best they could, only hers survived.

"But we still have each other," Vinh says, her voice as tight as a garrote. "We have each other, and that's all that matters."

029

Jacksonhaven didn't just take gestation chambers. They targeted the entire reproduction center. In vitro fertilization is impossible. The rival colony destroyed the fertility drugs needed to stimulate ova, the follicular aspiration needles required to remove them, the specialized culture medium necessary to support zygote growth, and the soft catheters used to implant embryos into uteruses.

The council of New Belaforme, in its infinite wisdom, comes up with a solution in a month. Amara suspects they decided after a handful of days, if that. The rest of the time was spent figuring out how to sugarcoat it.

Like everyone else, Amara is summoned to a ten-minute appointment in one of the private council chambers. She walks in at the precise assigned time, just after the noon gong. Councilwoman Margaret Choroba is already seated at the nondescript metallic table, manicured hands folded over the cool matte surface. She's probably already done this fifty times today, judging by the vacant look in her hazel eyes.

Amara sits down, her palms slippery with sweat. The settlers have all been sworn to silence until the end of the day, but she has her guesses, each worse than the last. Margaret waves a hand and the table spits out a hologram of Jesse's face. It's a good picture; Amara took it. The sun catches in his honey-blond hair; his turquoise-blue eyes match the exact shade of the cloudless sky above. Margaret smiles. She probably thinks the Council did Amara a favor. Amara and Jesse are already best friends. They're colleagues. They work well together in and outside of the lab. A not-insignificant number of people find Jesse attractive. Et cetera, et cetera.

Amara doesn't want Jesse. She wants Vinh. She knows for a fact that Jesse doesn't want her, probably even less than she wants him. They've known each other since their late teens, and Jesse has never *wanted* anyone like that. Ever.

"I don't understand," says Amara. "I thought we were in danger of starving."

"In the long term, if we aren't granted resources from the polity ship," Margaret replies smoothly. "Right now, our greatest danger is being deemed unproductive. The most important criteria for that has always been projected population growth."

"You don't have to do this," says Amara.

"We all must do our duty." Margaret won't meet her eyes now. "You're compatible. What do you want me to say? Is there someone else you'd prefer, someone who . . . would work?"

Amara stares at her. She has never thought of herself in such biological terms. In much of her original polity, medicine made sex such a mutable thing. The Ọ̀yọ́an idea of gender is equally flexible. Inconsequential, almost. (They don't have the necessary toolkit to make rapid, whole-body alterations here yet, and that's unlikely to change now; the required drugs and biotech are typically deemed nonessential for new colonies.)

Amara is a *she*—and female—only because it made sense when she came of age. Before the ceremony, her immediate family consisted of two mothers, a father, a partner set to marry in the moment a couple of corporate mergers went through and he got rid of his girlfriend, two siblings who used a variety of pronouns, two brothers, and one daughter. Amara has always liked balance. She contains multitudes, and to be reduced to the mere meat of her body—the original body she kept on nothing more than a whim—is uncomfortable. Deeply so.

"Fine, but . . ." Her voice shakes, just a little. She tries to steady it before continuing. "I don't have to marry or live with someone else to have children with them."

Margaret looks down at her hands for a long moment. "If everyone was allowed to remain solely with their spouses, how many do you think would actually do as we ask in the time we ask them to do it? You can continue to live with Vinh, eventually, but you'll cohabitate with her partner too."

"Have you considered an intrauterine option?" Amara asks. It's a much a simpler fertilization procedure than IVF; they should be able to make do with the medical equipment that survived the raid.

"We have. And if that's what you'd like to do, you can." Margaret's fingers curl inward for a second, as if she's about to ball them into fists, but she stops herself. "However, the Council believes that new, cohesive families will be good for raising whatever children are born."

"Who, exactly, believes that?"

"I'm not at liberty to say. But the restoration of, ah, former legal partnerships and living situations will be an option for citizens who demonstrate a high level of . . . cooperation."

First the carrot, and then the stick. The freedom of choice they're offering is theoretical. Amara bites the inside of her cheek until she tastes copper.

"I want you to know that I argued against it," Margaret says. Her words are nearly a whisper. "I was overruled."

Amara takes two deep breaths before she says, *"Fine. I will do whatever the Council deems necessary for the survival of New Belaforme."*

What else can she say? What else can she do? She has to put the settlement ahead of herself. She's struggled to do the right thing in the past, but this concerns the fate of her new home. All her work to protect New Belaforme means less than nothing if she doesn't do her part to save its future. She'll find some way around participating in the Council's breeding program, if she can, but fighting the councilors will only harden their minds toward her and make doing her actual job difficult. Besides, pushing back publicly on this point might incite others to rebellion, others who would otherwise bow their heads and do as the Council commands. Amara understands the need to expand their population as quickly as possible to remain in the Primacy's favor.

She's just going to leave that task to those better suited for it.

028

Henry's generously freckled cheeks go fire-red the moment he lays eyes on Vinh. It's endearing, almost, to see a thirtysomething-year-old man blush so deeply. It's been a while since she's gotten a reaction like that.

"Um, hello," he says, extending a hand. They're about the same height, but he looks up at her all the same. "How are you?"

Vinh has to laugh. "I'm fine," she says, and it's not even a complete lie, "all things considered. You?"

"Good. I mean, fine." He lets his hand, unshaken, drop. His eyes meet hers, flicking away again for half a second. "This is embarrassing, but I'm a huge fan of yours. I can't believe they matched us."

A . . . fan?

Of what, murder?

Vinh forces her smile to stay on her face. "My wife and I are monogamous, by the way. And even if I wanted to betray her, Amara would have my head."

Henry swallows visibly. His chin tips down and up in a stiff nod. "I understand," he says, and there's a dejected sigh behind the words. "But what about the Council?"

Vinh leans forward. "Between you and me," she whispers, all conspiratorial-like, "I'm exempt."

"They said so? That's not what—"

"I say so." Vinh feels her smile stretch, almost of its own accord. She reaches over, pumps his hand up and down in a firm shake. "Pleasure to meet you, Henry."

027

While a small army of the remaining robots invade Amara's home and begin moving her personal belongings to Jesse's house, she tells him, "Don't worry. We'll figure something out." Some way to keep the Council off their backs. Some way to make this work, to rescue and preserve whatever remains of their past lives.

The next day, the Council "strongly encourages" Amara to meet Vinh's new partner, Henry. They were assigned to each other with the same amount of pomp and fanfare as every other couple. Less than twenty-four hours ago, Amara and Vinh walked into the Council chambers as wives. They left, officially, as something legally less. In any case, the esteemed leaders of the colony want everyone to be on "good terms." Amara finds herself cautiously optimistic. It's not a complete surprise; her bàbá threw a hissy fit when First-ìyá declared her intention to have one of the family rivals marry in, but once everyone actually met in person, they all got along swimmingly.

Henry is taller than Amara but shorter than Vinh. His looks are slightly below average—stringy brown hair, watery green eyes, skin the dull color of limestone chalk. It's petty and shallow, and she feels awful for thinking it, but Amara takes great pleasure in knowing Henry has no chance of winning Vinh's affections. (Also, he has exactly twenty-three facial freckles, which is, objectively, a suboptimal number of freckles.)

Other than that, he's perfectly fine. Polite, a little shy. Inoffensive. She can make this work.

Still. When Vinh wraps her arms around Amara, so tight neither of them can breathe, it feels like it's for the last time. Amara whispers, "I don't want to go." What she means is *I don't want to live without you.*

"You know you don't have to," Vinh murmurs. "Just stay. Please."

Amara shakes her head, saying nothing. Better to go of her own accord, than be dragged out screaming by peace officers.

When Amara shows up at Jesse's house that night, he tells her to take the bed and passes out on the couch in the living room. Or at least he pretends to. Amara can neither find sleep nor affect it. She already feels like Vinh is slipping through her fingers. As the moons rise in the star-speckled sky, Amara promises herself, *If we don't survive this, neither will they.*

BEFORE

Amara is standing by the window, watching a lone skiff cleave through the snow outside, when Jesse comes in. She turns around wordlessly, looking over his pale, barefoot shape. She first met the man she now calls her closest friend on a station run by people from a desert world orbiting two suns. They kept the lights blinding and the heat scorching. Then, Jesse had a golden complexion and artificial sun-bleached blond hair. Now he matches the lifeless gray shade of his tunic and trousers.

"You look worse than I do," Amara quips. Her eyes ache from the tears she's shed over the past few days; she can only imagine how red and puffy they are.

Jesse sighs, a little exasperated puff of air. "Sit down," he says simply.

Once, Amara mistook the abrupt, straightforward manner he takes with her when they're alone for a deep dislike. She knows better now; Jesse is most taciturn with those he's fondest of. He stares into her eyes, his gaze unnervingly direct. After a moment, she falls into one of the two plush white chairs in the room. He takes the other, offering her a mug of the burnt bean juice that passes for a beverage on this planet. Amara forces down a mouthful of the acrid brew. Whoever decided *this* affront was a delicacy obviously didn't have taste buds.

"It's beautiful here," she says around the bitter taste, her gaze returning to the window.

Fresh powder flies in fluid, shimmering streams around the bow of the skiff as it slips out of view. The snow-blanketed ice is pristine and perfect, an infinite skein of featureless, bone-white silk. Above hangs the cloudless, crystal-blue vault of the sky.

Amara's parents have told her all the horror stories about new settlements. (Just last month, Buonaparte-Soto Incorporated tried to conscript the recently abandoned people of Léopol II as forced laborers, only for a navigational error to send the slave ships into who-knows-where.) Who could've anticipated that this chunk of ice and rock would become such a prized jewel? The planet's just large enough to have something approaching standard Earth gravity, which is nice, but it's too near the far edge of its star's circumstellar habitable zone to comfortably support life, including humans. Even for a polity as powerful as Noble Francia, Etretat II was a gamble—more so than colonies usually are. Deep-space settlement efforts are always shots in the dark, and sometimes bullets are lost to the endless black. Such is the nature of the alien beast.

"It wasn't always," Jesse says quietly. "Beautiful."

He's told her stories too, though far fewer. Etretat II failed as a mining outpost and nearly failed as a colony, before Noble Francia decided to turn it into a tourist resort. But that was all when Jesse was a boy; he barely remembers the hard days. At least, that's what he says.

"You can't hide here forever," Jesse says. "And you can't ignore her forever."

Amara's mouth twists. Her hands tighten around the mug. Of course, the time she most desires his silence is the time he gives her the least of it.

"I can and I will." She knows she sounds petulant. She can't help it.

"I won't let you," he replies, merciless as a blizzard. "She's my friend too."

"*I* was going to marry her," Amara snarls back, just as sharply. "She left without a word, Jesse." She slams the mug onto the low table between them before she has a chance to throw it. "She just packed up her things and left. I thought . . . I thought she went back to that lying bitch from Ak'e XIII."

"She told you it was a clean break."

"Yes, that's what she *told* me. She acted differently. I could tell she still felt something for him, weeks into our relationship."

Jesse lifts his eyes to the ceiling. "Well, she's back now. For good."

When Amara showed up at his door, sobbing her guts out, he took her in without a word. He's been taking care of her in a way her own family never did, making sure she gets enough food and sleep and company every day. But he's completely refused to entertain Amara's anger at *her*. At Vinh. She doesn't know whether to loathe or love him for it.

"I wasn't sure how to word this," Jesse says slowly, "but nothing else I've told you has gotten through, so . . ."

Truth be told, Amara barely recalls what he's told her thus far. Something about forgiveness, another thing about patience. The moment his voice takes on the half-pleading, half-exasperated tone it does now, she starts to drift away. Today, though, she'll do her best to listen. She owes him her ear, at the very least.

". . . I'm just going to say it."

Surprise swallows Amara's anger. She's never known a single sentence to leave Jesse's mouth without a great deal of thought. "Well?"

He clasps his hands over his knees. She can almost see the frustration rolling off his shoulders. "Have you tried to consider why Vinh left you?"

In less than a second, Amara's outrage returns, doubled. Her teeth grind together. "How dare you? I haven't thought of anything else but why—"

"You haven't." Jesse drags in a deep breath. "Allow me to remind you that your second-ìyá served an unprecedented *three* terms as the Supreme Chancellor of Great Ọ̀yọ́. Allow me to remind you that your family can trace its lineage to one of the founding families of a capital planet. You're practically a princess."

"I'm aware," Amara drawls, her voice tight behind the feigned nonchalance. She wrestles with her own hands, forcing them to remain flat at her sides rather than turn into fists. She doesn't know what she'd do with them, if they did. Family has always been a delicate subject for her, to say the least.

"Are you, though?" Jesse arches a brow. "Meanwhile, Vinh's home settlement didn't even have a name until it became profitable enough for Vạn Xuân."

Amara waves a dismissive hand, increasingly uncomfortable. "That's just standard procedure. Vạn Xuân doesn't name any colonies until they're deemed successful."

"Are you hearing yourself right now?" Jesse's voice raises for the first time Amara has witnessed. "Your parents were going to have her *assassinated* so you could marry that tech mogul's daughter."

"I thought you weren't one for dramatics," Amara says lowly. "I'd never let them touch her."

"The only real drama is the one you dragged her into." He forges on into Amara's stunned silence. "All that matters is that she *believed* they might really get rid of her that time, regardless of whatever you might say or want or do. Give her another chance."

"She broke my heart, Jesse."

"Hearts can mend." He says it so simply.

"Not when they're shattered." Jesse makes a face, which she ignores. "And as you have so condescendingly explained to me," Amara says slowly, "it's complicated."

"No, it isn't."

"You're not making any sense."

"It's not complicated."

Amara narrows her eyes. Her patience is wearing atom-thin.

"The *galaxy* is complicated," Jesse says. "*Politics* are complicated. But that's behind you now. Your family finally let you go." He pulls a heavy tome from the table and opens it up to the bookmarked page. "So now you have two very simple questions to answer. Could you ever be happy without her? And would you be happy with her?"

"Those aren't simple questions."

"And yet, I think you know the answers."

Amara looks again to the view. The last of the day's sunlight bleeds weakly across the darkening sky, but the snow seems to gleam even brighter.

He's right, of course. She's finally, finally free. So is Vinh. If Amara could only forgive her . . . They could do anything, be anything. These days, untouched habitable planets are being found faster than they can be claimed. Manifest Destiny—that's what the settlers of yore called it. The three of them could start a new settlement together, build something as glorious as Etretat II from the ground up. It'll be a hard life at first, with great danger at every turn. But it's the cost of something that makes it beautiful. Her relationship with Vinh was . . . *is* much the same.

026

There are flowers on the doorstep of Jesse's house. Amara picks them up and drags in a deep breath. There's even a card, too. Handwritten.

From: Henry, To: Amara.

Hmm.

She tucks the slip of paper into her back pocket and brings the bouquet to her face again. The common name the botanists decided on is the spotted pinkpuff. They're pretty things: gold-freckled flowers and spiraling silver-green stems. Their perfume is faint; she has to really stick her nose in the bouquet to catch the scent. It's lovely. So delicate. They don't sell these in stores because they're so finicky once cut, and they haven't figured out how to stop them from wilting in a day. Henry must've gone on a stroll and picked them himself.

If Amara were a jealous, paranoid person, she'd probably think this was . . . what? Some sort of power play? Henry trying to convince them he's all nice and sweet, so Vinh will like him? So Amara will mind less while he tries to get her wife into bed? Thankfully, Amara is not a jealous, paranoid person. She understands that this is an honest gesture. So she walks back inside, snatches up her talkglass, and calls Henry to express her gratitude. She has to meet him halfway. She can't let him be better than her, either.

"Thanks for the flowers," she says, turning into the kitchen.

"You like them?"

She selects a cobalt-blue vase and fills it with water. "Very much."

"Oh, I'm so glad. Vinh told me they're one of your favorite flowers."

Amara says nothing as she drops the pinkpuffs, one by one, into the vase. She has to be mindful of the needlelike thorns. "Look, Henry, we're going to be in each other's lives for the foreseeable future. I'm thinking we ought to get to know each other a bit. We should . . . We should get dinner sometime, all four of us."

"Oh, I'd like that, Amara. I really would." A nervous sound, almost a giggle. "Y'know, I thought you hated me, for a second there. The day we met."

"Maybe for a second," Amara says, smiling. "But this isn't your fault. You're not all that bad." She forges on before he can respond to that. "Is there any place in particular you want to go?"

"Well, they'd just finished building this Kawkawi-Belaforman fusion spot before . . ." Before Jacksonhaven attacked. "It's been on my list for a hot minute."

"Perfect," Amara says. "Let me know when, and I'll tell Jesse."

"I'm looking forward to it," says Henry. "Thanks."

"No," says Amara, bending down to take another sniff, "thank you. The flowers are lovely."

"This is a bad idea," says Jesse. Right now he's sitting at the bottom of the stairs leading to his bedroom.

"It's a great idea." Amara crouches before the foyer shoe rack, surveying her options. "The best idea, really."

"Don't say I didn't warn you."

Now Amara turns on him. "I'm doing exactly what you told me to do. I'm making nice. I'm adapting."

"Hmm."

"Maybe if I get to know him a bit, I'll want him to die screaming a little less." She rolls her eyes when he frowns. "Lighten up, my gods. It was a joke." Under her breath: "Obviously."

"Hmm."

She finally makes a decision and slips on a pair of patent leather stilettos. "There's no ulterior motive, Jesse."

"Yeah, that's what I'm worried about. I think you're looking for one, and this is good fodder, kindling, whatever you want to call it."

She turns this way and that in front of the hallway mirror, admiring the way the creaseless black fabric of her dress hugs her curves. The fabric is incredibly breathable, lighter than cotton and smoother than silk. The bovid that produces the wool went extinct on its native planet a century ago; all that remains are a few heavily guarded caches of its fleece. There's de-extinction technology, of course, but bringing the species back would render the stores worthless and tank the market, so. What she's wearing is a monstrosity of sorts, but it was a birthday gift from her then-soon-to-be second-bàbá, so she figures it's okay. She would never have purchased such a thing herself.

"How do I look?"

"Symmetrical." Jesse picks up her favorite coat, a long scarlet confection with mother-of-pearl buttons.

"I don't need that," Amara says, fiddling with the clasp of her necklace. "It's spring. And we live in the tropical zone, let me remind you."

He folds the coat over his arm, running his fingers over the embroidered cuffs to smooth them. "The restaurant maintains a constant indoor temperature of nineteen degrees Celsius. The receptionist said they keep the room a little cool to keep their guests alert, and therefore better able to 'appreciate the artistry of the dishes.'"

"Pretentious fucks."

"Yes, I know. You know what else I know?" Jesse steps forward and, without ever touching her skin, fastens the dainty loop of diamonds behind her neck. He arches a brow at her in the mirror. "You're most comfortable at a balmy twenty-one degrees. You'll need the coat. Now can we please go? On time is late."

Normally Amara would be approximately as anal about timing as Jesse, but she just checked Vinh's location. She grabs her purse with an indulgent smile. "Don't get your panties in a bunch. We'll get there long before they do."

She checks her lipstick one last time, and then they're off. As Amara anticipated, Vinh and Henry arrive a few minutes after they do, right on time. Vinh's wearing the tailored silk suit Amara bought her two years after they officially started dating. It fit her beautifully then, and it fits her beautifully now. She looks good.

Really, really good.

Henry checks in for them. Amara follows the group to their table on autopilot. She can't keep her eyes off her wife.

Their waiter is a friendly young man named Ben. He skips up to their table, talkglass in hand and so very eager to start off with drinks. The soup of the day, perhaps? It's an excellent chowder, made from 100 percent local ingredients. Not a single reconstituted Earth-descended potato to be found, no ma'am—

"We'll get four bowls," Amara interrupts. "And bread, if you don't charge extra." She could afford it otherwise, obviously. They all could, except maybe Henry; she has no idea what he does for a living. But it's the principle of the thing.

"I'm so sorry, unfortunately we do," murmurs Ben. He looks mildly embarrassed; he's good.

"But you can't have chowder without bread," says Henry. He winks at Amara—what is *that* supposed to mean?—and turns to Ben. "A basket, please."

"I'll get that right away," says Ben, and he does. By the time he returns, they've perused the menu sufficiently and they're ready to order.

When Ben practically pirouettes away again, Henry excuses himself for a moment to go wash his hands. Amara and Jesse, being enlightened and also generally better than Henry, produce tiny glass dispensers of scentless hand sanitizer and spritz their hands. Amara holds her bottle out across the table.

"He really likes you," Vinh says, putting out her hands.

Amara coats her wife's palms with a generous helping of isopropyl alcohol. "Hmm."

A muscle in Vinh's cheek flinches. "He wants to impress you, Amara."

"Hmm."

"I'm sorry," says Vinh.

Amara starts, looking up in concern. She wasn't being serious. "Why are you apologizing?"

Vinh's shoulders rise in a minuscule shrug. She looks like someone's just spat in her water.

When Henry comes back, Amara says, "What do you think about us all moving in together?"

"I'd really like that," Vinh says softly. "We'll have to apply for group housing, and couples with children will get priority, but yeah . . . I'd really, really like that."

"And what about you, Henry?" Amara asks.

Henry blinks. "Sure!" he says, but the cheer in his tone rings false. "If you're fine with that."

Of course, Amara thinks wryly. *Of course he wants all of Vinh all to himself.* So, as it turns out, they have something in common after all.

"Why wouldn't I be fine with that?" she asks.

"I don't know."

"Well, I suggested it, didn't I?"

Their food arrives. Jesse, in a surprising show of charisma, carries most of the following conversation, with friendly, dull-eyed responses from Henry, occasional interjections from Amara, and a comment here and there from Vinh, who keeps glancing over. Amara notes each furtive look with exponentially increasing satisfaction. Consuming dinner, dessert, and a bottle of wine takes precisely one hour, fifteen minutes, and fifty-nine seconds. As soon as Amara drains the final mouthful in her glass and Henry scrapes the last bit of chocolate ganache from his dish, Jesse wisely flags down Ben and gracefully parries all attempts from Vinh and Henry to split the bill.

They say their goodbyes. Jesse and Henry shake hands; Amara reaches up for the glossy lapels of Vinh's suit, tugs her down, and presses their mouths together, hard. Vinh's soft and reciprocating—only for a moment. Amara literally feels her wife realize: they're in public, someone's probably going to tell one of the Council's cronies, and Henry is still *right there.* The way Vinh's eyes fly open stings. They're married, for fuck's sake.

Or they were.

Vinh steps away with an uneven laugh. "Um. Well. You could just say you missed me."

"I missed you," Amara says shortly, and then she turns on her heel.

Jesse follows. He gives Amara a sad little smile as they head toward the path home. He doesn't say what they're both thinking. She doesn't deserve him. Never has, and probably never will.

025

Progress is not being made at the rate needed to meet the minimum population requirements of a success-ful colony in half a millennium. There will be a two-year grace period. New couples who do not produce at least one offspring after that will be reassigned.

024

So, not to pry, I'm just curious," Henry starts, one hand already raised placatingly (Vinh rolls her eyes) as he pads into the living room with a fresh bottle of wine, "what's the long-term plan here?"

Vinh sighs, smiles, rolls her shoulders. "Oh, simple. If anyone dares to follow up on us, I'll just level some threats, break a few fingers as necessary. Nothing serious. You know, the usual."

She's never so brutally blunt with Amara. It feels refreshing, to speak honestly of violence. Or rather, her capacity for it. Vinh *is* the job. They picked her because she's a dangerous woman. With Henry, she doesn't have to pretend differently.

Henry looks a tad green as he refills Vinh's glass. "You know, I have a friend in the medical sector. We could just call him and ask."

Vinh arches a brow, but she waves an assenting hand. "Fine, we'll try it your way first. Just let me finish my pinot."

He sets up the workglass inlaid into the coffee table as she sips. She never really liked wine, until Amara introduced her to it.

Henry's "friend" is Calais Thom, a mid-tier physician. Vinh met the man once, during the second or third introductory rounds, but this is her first real interaction with him. He starts speaking before she can even get a half-polite greeting out.

"Vinh, why are *you* calling?" His deeply furrowed brows sit like two great brown caterpillars over unnervingly bright eyes.

Henry leans over at Vinh's side, his head popping onto the screen.

"Oh," says Calais. "I see." He starts laughing.

Vinh waits patiently, blunt nails digging into her palms. "What's so funny?"

Calais stops laughing immediately. Clever boy. "Well, obviously the orders don't extend to *you*. You're head of security, and no one's qualified to replace you." He snorts, curving two neatly manicured hands over a vast imaginary belly. "You can't fight if you're knocked up! Just don't advertise that you get special treatment, please and thank you."

Vinh's left eye twitches.

Calais turns to Henry. "It wouldn't hurt to let the boys know how happy you are with your assignment, if you catch my meaning. Doctor's orders."

"Er," says Henry.

"No, he's right, go ahead," Vinh says. She grins at the doctor. "I won't forget this, Calais."

She hangs up.

023

There's a fruit on the planet—tentative taxonomic name: *Kalleesia duvasima*—much beloved by a species of mildly disagreeable rust-furred scorpion-adjacent animals. But the beasts don't go after the fruit, no. The flesh is bitter, unpalatable. They crave the sweet, tender seeds inside, and the tree, reproductively speaking, craves not having its seeds eaten. Countless years of intense coevolution later, the fruit has developed shells harder than concrete and an inner layer resembling the spiny glochidia of a cactus. The not-scorpions have gotten very, very good at manipulating sticks and stones to get at the goods.

The seeds are delicious, and Amara's favorite snack, and when she walks into the kitchen, there Jesse is with a pile of the fruit. He's cracking away at the shells, carefully scooping out the seeds with a slender instrument he bullied the fabrication techs into crafting for him before the raid.

"Well, shit," he says. "Surprise ruined."

His smiles are so very exact. Mathematically perfect. Amara's hands itch for a protractor.

"Not ruined," she says, not getting the protractor because she is normal. After a moment of hesitation, she slides onto the bar stool opposite him. She's not quite sure what to do with him these days. They've never actually cohabitated before. She says her next words very carefully, testing the waters. "Thanks. You know, you're not so bad at the whole spouse thing, all things considered."

Jesse makes a completely immature retching noise, and suddenly everything's easy again. Amara laughs, plants her elbows on the granite island, and tucks into the bowl of plump seeds.

"I mean it," she says between bites. "Thank you."

Jesse rolls his eyes and cracks open another fruit. "It's nothing. Nothing at all."

022

Amara and Vinh meet whenever they can. The Council isn't foolish enough to try to outlaw former spouses from seeing each other, but they emphasize, over and over and over, the importance of investing as much energy and time into their new relationships as possible.

The women sit on a handwoven blanket on a hill, their backs against the wide, orange trunk of a tree. Together they watch the sun sink below the mountains. The star is slightly warmer than Earth's and slightly cooler than Cristoffa Prime's.

"It could be worse," says Vinh. "They could've paired me with Desmond. Can you imagine?" She presses a hand over her heart, her voice pitched for maximum drama.

Amara forces a laugh as she selects a local date-analogue from the charcuterie board between them.

It could be worse. She knows that. Good people died in the raid. If Vinh had been there, peerless fighter though she is, she could've been hurt. But that doesn't make Amara feel better about losing her marriage. They're together, but only in the stolen moments between when they aren't.

(*Again, where the hells did she go that night?* Amara has asked three times now, and gotten increasingly flippant answers for her efforts.)

"Henry isn't so bad, actually," Vinh murmurs, sipping the

last of her champagne. "Under other circumstances, I could grow to like him, maybe. You could too, Amara, if you gave him half a chance."

"I *have*," Amara says. "I *am*."

She's never loathed anyone before, not truly. She feels like she's starting to despise Vinh's so-called husband a bit, even though she knows he doesn't really deserve her hatred. But holding on to her sympathy for him and his impossible situation is like trying to hold on to a handful of smoke. At some point, she has to ask herself why she should bother. Which, of course, makes her feel even worse. Their application for group housing is about to go up for evaluation, but the truth is, she thinks she'd rather live apart from Vinh than sleep under the same roof as Henry.

The grace period is already half-over. Everyone else seems to be making *progress*, and the four of them are running out of time. Many of the couples, new and old, have managed to make this work. They willingly share their original partners. A number of pairs, maybe most, have formed stable poly-cules, moving into the same houses and raising their off-spring together. Some were in polyamorous relationships when they signed up in the first place, or began them on-world long before the Council offered its "solution." And, of course, there's Amara's own family back in Great Ọyọ́. It's not like she doesn't have ample examples of how to make this work.

I could grow to like him, maybe.

Vinh and the rest of the settlement are trying to make the best of their new lives, and Amara just . . . isn't. As is her biannual ritual, she recently compiled a spreadsheet logging her daily activities in fifteen-minute intervals for a week. There's no escaping the truth when it's in crisp numbers: when she's not working, all she does is wallow and whine and want. Well, mostly. She attends the required weekly fertility appointments, where one of the physicians drones on and on about what she already knows she should be doing and how. She must stop drinking ("Seriously, I am not joking, Amara."), she must cut down on caffeine, she must not forget the folic acid supplements. Exercise while maintaining a stable weight. Sleep eight hours. Stop being so stressed. And timing is everything—they're giving her ovulation test strips for a reason. Et cetera. (Jesse, supportive partner that he is, plays video games on his talkglass outside. She supposes she should be grateful he even bothers to show up.)

For a while, Amara played the part of the dutiful wife well enough. She nodded along and lied through her teeth about how she and Jesse spent their evenings. As the head biologist, she's technically part of the colony's administration. They trust her. Others have not been so lucky, but that's not really her problem.

Then a physician commented on how well both she and Vinh seemed to be taking it all. While he praised Amara's seeming sense of duty, he commented on Vinh and Henry's apparent *enthusiasm*. Amara nearly gave him a black eye on the way out.

I could grow to like him.

She wants Vinh to hate Henry. Just a little. She wants Vinh to run away with her, wants Vinh to want her more than the future of the settlement. She knows exactly how selfish that is, how hypocritical she's being, but that doesn't make her desire any of those things an iota less.

If Vinh and Henry had a child together, could she love it, if the Council let them all raise the baby together? The answer her brain immediately supplies is not a good one.

Amara wants to be happy for Vinh. And Henry. She wants to be consoled by the unassailable fact that the woman she loves has found comfort in another person, when Amara herself can't be there for her in the way she wants to. But every time she tries to summon a positive emotion, she feels liquid nitrogen pour into her stomach. The coolant burns right through her, setting her mouth afire with frostbite and perforating her gastrointestinal tract. She is *not* being melodramatic.

I like him.

She knows her relationship with Vinh, even at the best of times, wasn't, isn't, perfect. All she can think of now is how their chance to fix things—to really fix things—was stolen. The colony must always come first, but there must've been a better way. She's just too weak, too much of a coward, to see it. Stomach acid rises up Amara's throat, sharp and sweetly sour. She wants to scream. Or cry. She's not sure. The only thing she knows for certain is that some awful feeling is building in her chest and behind her eyes. She can't do this anymore.

The first step to *loving* is *liking*.

One day, someday, *I like him* might be *I love him*.

Amara shoots to her feet.

"Amara, what—" Vinh reaches for her, uncharacteristically slow. "Did I say something wrong?"

Amara's breaths come fast and shallow as she starts walking back to Jesse's home. Not their home, or hers. It will never be hers.

"Wait, come back!" Vinh calls. "What did I do? I'm sorry!"

Amara doesn't turn back. She can't. The tears are already streaming down her face.

021

Vinh strides into her home office, power and purpose thrumming in her veins. She sets down her talkglass and a tall glass of water on the desk. She lowers herself into her chair and wipes the sweat from her hands onto her jeans. She drags in a deep breath, filling her lungs until they burn, and then lets it go. She takes a sip of water, wetting her parched throat. She is ready. She extends an arm and lifts her talkglass. Her heartbeat is already picking up again as she pulls up the desired contact.

Fucking hell.

It's just Amara. Her *wife*.

Vinh feels like an appropriate amount of time has passed to figure out whatever the fuck went down on that hill. Twenty-four hours is enough, right? (*Right?*) Better to reach out now than to have Jesse force her. Amara doesn't answer on the first ring, or the second. It's hardly the first missed call between them, but . . .

Suddenly, without warning, Vinh is ten again, and her parents are telling her why Bác Huy hasn't been answering the talkglass. Why he won't answer the talkglass, ever again. Bác Huy made the best cá kho tộ she'd ever tasted, laughed with his whole belly, and always brought her sweets. But first and foremost, he was a proud man, and his pride got his immediate family killed. He was part of the second colonization wave on New Hội An's second moon. When Bác Huy had uprooted his quarter of the family and taken them away to be part of a better, brighter future, the burgeoning colony had been doing so well. Then, suddenly, it hadn't.

When things *had* been good, he'd called once a week, oftentimes only to brag. As corporate infighting slowly tore apart the rare-earth-metal mining operations at the seams, his calls started to come only a few times a year, and only then to beg for spare credits. Then he'd cut off contact, just as the news stations began to report that the two heir presumptives of Apex Metals were sending hired muscle after each other.

The storm-cloud-gray lunar dust drank up the blood of those who died. Still, the violence had been minimal, and targeted. Rescue of the vast majority of the colony was possible, but the heirs were both dead, and relief efforts were deemed unprofitable. That wasn't the official story, but it was the truth everyone knew. And so loved ones fell silent, one by one.

Vinh hears the front door slide open. Before she knows what she's doing, she's fled to the bathroom across the hall and locked the door.

"Henry?"

There's a long silence. Then comes Amara's voice, threaded with her usual knife-sharp concern. "Sorry I didn't pick up, my talkglass died and I—"

Vinh leans her head against the cool surface of the door, trying to keep her heaving sobs silent. A hand clamped over her mouth isn't enough, so she bites down on her fist until she tastes blood. Bones grind between her teeth. But she can't let her wife hear, or see, how she's fallen to pieces over a single unanswered call. All Amara knows about Bác Huy is that he's the stubborn uncle who insisted on cooking elaborate holiday feasts, on all the kids learning calligraphy, on

Vinh's historically masculine name because he just liked the sound so much. Vinh never told Amara about the final failed colony. She never wants to need comfort from her wife. *She must be the strong one. Her support is all she has to offer.*

"Vinh?" A faint knock, light as a raindrop. "I'm sorry I left things like that yesterday. I shouldn't have just . . . Are you all right?"

She swallows, stumbling back from the door. "Yeah. Yeah. Just give me a moment."

"You don't sound all right." Amara's voice is softer than rose petals. "Let me in?"

"No!" It's so close to a shout. Too close. "No, I'm fine. Sorry. I'm fine."

"Vinh." Is that suspicion in her tone? "*Please.* Talk to me."

Vinh pries open her mouth to speak, and it's the second-hardest thing she's ever done. "Why can't you ever, *ever* leave well enough alone? I said, *give me a moment.*"

That's all it takes. If there's one thing Vinh's naturally good at, it's wounding her wife with only a handful of words.

"Okay." An uneven breath. "I'm going to— Just . . . I'm sorry, Vinh." And then she's gone.

020

The deep forest gets louder at night. Or at least it seems to, without human-generated noise to drown out the sounds of invisible animals snorting and slithering and singing in the darkness. If she closes her eyes—which she won't, because she can't—she can almost pretend she's not about to do what she's about to do. The cawing of some birdlike creature all but drowns out the muffled, begging sobs of the man at her feet.

He's gagged, but she understands him well enough. She can see the plea in his reddened eyes.

Please, he's saying. *Please. Don't do this.*

It's funny how people never expect they're going to die until they do. Despite the dead bodies piled up around them (nice and neat and already prepped for swift disposal), despite the New Belaforme security officers standing at attention with smoking guns . . . Behind the raw terror and healthy dose of rage in his broken expression is one last, desperate glint of hope—but no one and nothing is coming for him, just death. The corpses and her officers fade. Then it's just her, and him, and the gun.

Please. I have a family.

The horrible, bitter part of her she's always had to shove into a hole around her wife answers, *I don't want your family.* She just wants to get back to her own. Vinh shakes her head once, lifting her arm.

"Orders are orders," she says. She knows it'll be a cold comfort but she can't stop the words now that they're out. "I'm sorry."

She tries not to make a habit of lying, but any leader has to make exceptions. She took a vow. She swore an oath to protect the colony. To protect Amara. She *is* sorry, though. As much as she ever is, in times like these. She always does what needs to be done.

Just as she presses the muzzle to the prisoner's sweat-stained, dirt-smeared temple, he . . . changes. His form shimmers and shifts, like a distant figure obscured by heat waves. There's someone else kneeling in his place now.

It's *her*.

Amara smiles, her teeth pinked with blood. "Oh, darling," she croons. "What's wrong?"

Vinh gasps—or tries to. She chokes on the intake of air, and all that comes out of her throat is a garbled whimper, like the prisoner. She jerks her arm back, taking the pistol with it. "Amara—"

Amara lurches forward, as much as she can with her limbs lashed behind her. She presses her forehead to the muzzle. She twists her head to the side, so Vinh can see the sharp white fullness of her grin.

"Do it," she demands. "I know you want to." Then she laughs, like it's all some sick joke, like they're having one of those fights they refuse to accept is a fight.

Vinh tries to fling aside the pistol but she can't. Her fingers have frozen around the gun, caught in an icy rigor mortis. She's trembling.

"*Do it,*" Amara says again, and this time the words are soft and low and gentle, like when she wants to be kissed but is too proud to ask. Vinh always thought it was endearing. "I know you've wanted to."

"I don't." Vinh tastes the salt of her own tears. "Amara, please, I *don't*. I'd never—"

"Liar," Amara murmurs, her eyes half-lidded. "*Liar*. I see it when you think I'm not looking. I see it in your eyes."

Without warning, their positions reverse. Vinh sits crumpled at her wife's feet. The executed captives are back, dead save for their eyes. They watch, pupils dilating, as Amara raises the gun. Vinh tries to scream, but she's gagged. She wants to weep at the unfairness of it all. Why can't she ever have the last word?

Vinh meets Amara's loving gaze. She feels a thumb drag down her cheek, rough and bloodied. She doesn't have to look to know it's the nearest body, reaching up to pet her. Soft, wet fingers gently brush down her jaw. The fingernails are missing, torn away like hard little petals. They had tortured the captives first. The clean, coppery tang of fresh blood fills Vinh's lungs. A little mewl escapes from between clenched teeth. She can't explain it, can't glance down to confirm, but somehow she's knows that the body is Amara, too.

"It's okay," the first Amara whispers, a secret just for them. The muzzle is a brand between Vinh's brows. "I want it too."

She pulls the trigger, and the corpse goes in for a kiss.

Vinh's eyes fly open, her gritted teeth unlocking to release a noiseless cry. She wants to sob like in that wretched dream, but she's trained herself out of giving in to her weakness post-nightmare. Amara's always been such a light sleeper that she had to. You can make yourself do anything if you want it badly enough.

The mind controls the breath controls the heart controls the mind.

She repeats the pattern over and over like a prayer, forcing herself to think of nothing. When that doesn't work, she settles for thinking of anything but her wife blowing her brains out, and mostly succeeds. She takes deeper, longer breaths. Her heart stops its mad thrashing behind her ribs, slowing, and eventually—eventually—the panic subsides.

Mission accomplished. For now.

Vinh throws off the covers, weighing her options. She could get up, get a glass of water. Or maybe something stronger. She knows she's not getting any more sleep. She sits up, the cold air hitting her back like a bucket of Etretatian snow; she's soaked in sweat. Shivering, she slips out of bed and tiptoes to the closet. Ripping off her ratty old shirt, she digs around for another and yanks it on. Her movement is too fast, too sudden, her heartbeat ticks up a fraction of a second faster—

Mind, breath, heart, mind.

Mind.

Breath.

Heart.

Mind.

Her coiled muscles loosening, Vinh creeps into the kitchen, virtually silent. Unfortunately, it seems Henry is even easier to wake than her wife. He stumbles into the room just as she opens the liquor cabinet.

"Vinh?" He yawns, rubbing at his eyes. He blinks blearily, his gaze going from her probably wrecked face to the assorted bottles before her and then back. "Um."

She tries to swallow a groan, then she remembers. He isn't Amara. He's neither beyond nor better than her, so he can't expect perfection from her either. She doesn't have to try so hard. She lets the sound out.

"What's wrong?" Henry asks, suddenly and fully awake now.

"Nothing."

He walks over to the kitchen table and sits. He pushes out the chair next to him with his foot, a clear invitation.

"What's wrong?" he says, again. His tone is mild but his posture is stubborn.

Vinh says nothing for a moment. She closes the liquor cabinet, filling her mug with water instead of vodka. *He isn't Amara.* She joins him at the table, admitting defeat. She can be a little weak around him.

"I fucked up," she rasps. She hasn't taken so much as a sip yet; her throat feels impossibly dry, like she's choked back a handful of sand.

The inadequacy of the words only deepens her guilt. Can't she do anything right? She drops her head into her hands.

"Vinh," says Henry, almost pleading. "Talk to me."

She shakes her head violently, screwing her eyes shut. It's all her fault. She ruined it. She's destroyed them. Amara. New Belaforme. She's going to lose them both. She doesn't know how long she'll last without her wife, without her home, without her purpose. They're all the same thing. If she's lucky, she'll be the first to go—

"We all fuck up," Henry says, interrupting her spiraling.

Vinh looks up, finally, to find him offering her a sad smile.

"Not like this," she whispers. She couldn't make her voice louder if she tried.

The world was placed into her clumsy, cruel hands and now all that's left is ash. Everyone seems so certain that the settlement will make it through this mess if they all do their part, but Vinh knows better. No colony survives something this bad and nothing good survives her.

"We all fuck up," Henry repeats, firmer this time. "And yet here we are, still alive. You can't blame yourself for what Jacksonhaven did, or for what's happened after."

She doesn't feel like she's really, truly alive. Part of her is still trapped in that nightmare, caught between the press of her own pistol and the caress of the corpse. She lets him pat her shoulder, barely resisting the urge to brush him off. She tells herself again and again that she doesn't have to be good enough for him. She doesn't have to be good at all. She can let herself be as damaged and worthless as she really is, and he can't leave her. The Council said so.

She lets her eyes flutter closed, and tries to tell herself she believes him.

019

The arrowhead crashes to the forest floor, his six hooves skittering against the wet leaves. His skull knocks against the hard bark of a tree, and he unleashes a pathetic, panting trill. His eyes are wild as sweat pours off his speckled hide.

He knows what's coming.

The hunter, a red-blooded Jacksonhaven man born and bred, draws a knife from his belt. He brings the glinting tip not to one of the arrowhead's hearts for a mercy kill, but to the throat. The beautiful mane turns ruby-red as lifeblood sprays. The arrowhead screams and thrashes, kicking out desperately with all his legs. The hunter plants a knee in the creature's stomach and presses down. The arrowhead vomits up a little globule of Gray and breathes his last, shuddering breath.

The man continues sawing away. The blade slides between two pearly vertebrae, severing the cervical spine in a jagged cut. The hunter grabs the creature's head by one great gloved fistful of the mane, letting out a pleased hoot as he brings the wreck to his face.

"A beaut," he remarks, nodding to himself, and stuffs the head into a bag.

A trophy.

A trophy.

Not sustenance. Not necessity.

A trophy.

The world trembles, as if dying a little Itself, a tremor so minute the hunter does not, cannot, sense it. Only one human can and he cannot know what it means, not yet.

018

Amara's bàbá once told her that people could only hurt her if she let them. She'd argued, respectfully of course, that one couldn't love without vulnerability. At the time she was the favored heir—clever but obedient, ruthless but loyal. Her credentials glittered like stars in the sky, or the jewels gracing her ears and ankles. He replied that love was weakness, and that her duty as a member of the family was to be strong. She'd chafed at those callous words; up until that moment she'd hoped against hope that deep down, he cared for her. Now Amara sees how right he was. She ignored his counsel, and now she is weak and wanting and alone.

She shouldn't be doing this. She's doing it anyway.

Vinh's personal log isn't particularly difficult to hack. New Belaforme's system still has Amara registered as Vinh's partner, even though that's no longer officially recognized. She gets through the first three levels of security on status alone, and then all she has to do is guess a password. She already knows the numerical component—Vinh always tacks on her birth year. She gets it on the third attempt, after trying the names of Vinh's first pet (a cat; Smudge) and of her home-world settlement (New Hội An). It's the club they met at: Lê's. She felt stupid even typing it in, and the answer fills her with equal measures of pleasure and guilt. She is, after all, breaking into her wife's private journal.

Amara has no idea what to expect as she opens the last four entries. Maybe she wants, needs, to punish herself. She's been wallowing in a mire of alternating misery and anger ever since Vinh practically chased her out of *their* house two weeks ago. The only thing that's broken through was the form rejection for their group housing application, and thank the gods for that. But now she's running out of fuel, and a paragraph or two about how happy Vinh is with Henry will solve that problem. He's probably a better listener. Definitely a better cook. The bar is pretty low.

She swigs the bourbon in her hand, nearly draining it. She'll have to get up to refill it soon, but she's already having trouble sitting upright. How badly would she damage her ego by crawling across the floor for more booze? She flops back into the couch, pulls her workglass onto her lap, and starts reading.

The first two entries are mostly about New Hội An. Vinh misses her home, that much is clear. She writes about the glittering sunsets. The consistently humid weather, warm as a hug. The bánh bò nướng vendor who only ever appeared during festivals. According to the journal, the seller always said it was because it was nearly impossible to grow pandan for the spongy cakes on that planet, but Vinh suspects he only baked them a couple of times a year to drive up demand.

Nothing about Henry, which is both good and bad. Bad because the whole point of this awful exercise was to dig up something she could obsess over and whinge about for the next week. Good because she has no idea what self-destructive behavior she'd indulge in if Henry came up. There's nothing about Amara either, at first.

Then she starts on the third entry. Her heart flies into her throat as she reads the first line.

I don't know how to apologize to her. How do I tell her I left because I didn't deserve her? I still don't. She probably thinks it's because her father threatened to kill me. Again. Or maybe she doesn't; I don't think I ever told her how bad it got—I handled his thugs before, and I didn't want to worry her. Sometimes I have no clue what's going on in her head. She hides so much. We need to talk about it, about everything. But the words die on my tongue every time I open my mouth.

Thing is, he did it face-to-face this time. That means something. He told me he'd have me sent back to my family in pieces, which really wasn't very original. (Also: as if.) But the look in his eyes as he said it . . . He was begging me to just go. I saw then. He just wants the best for his little girl. And I'm not it.

She gave up everything for me. I had nothing to give up. She had billions to her name. Power, fame. Even if her family hadn't been her family, she would've been respected. She wouldn't have needed her last name to earn a tenure-track position at any university in any system. And there I was, barely making ends meet because I was always too proud to let her help. The security position for the Primacy was my only option. Bodyguards aren't in high demand these days, especially human ones, what with those stupid new androids.

She could have had anything she wanted. A life, for starters, and I took that. I wish I'd been strong enough to stay away. I almost did, went back and forth a couple times. Then I'd remember how she fought against her parents when they ordered us to part. Against shitty employers who wouldn't pay up when the job was done. She was there for me when no one even bothered to care.

I wish I didn't need her so much.
I wish I could let her go.

Amara cries out, chest heaving with the force of her sobs. She should never have doubted Vinh's feelings. She should have feared them, perhaps. She's never seen the truth so clearly: they're going to destroy each other, and they'll do it oh so sweetly. They'll carve out pieces of themselves to offer the other until there's nothing left. They'll consume each other until even their memory is gone. If Vinh can't leave her, then there's no hope of Amara being able to let go. Her jealousy, her bitterness—there's nothing nice in her without Vinh. But as long as they have each other, it doesn't really matter.

And yet already Amara's worries rise anew, her mind circling back to Henry. Vinh will always love her, she knows that now, but love can be shared. Scattered. First-ìyá valued Amara's second-ìyá and bàbá a little less after their fiancé moved in. It was only a small decrease in affection, but it was noticeable. Amara saw it in First-ìyá's eyes. She *saw* it. Vinh may take the better path, and Amara fears that more than the colony's probably impending end. Tears carve burning rivulets in her cheeks as she slides to the next page. But there isn't any more; the next entry begins to load.

The captives keep insisting they're scientists, but they're basically digging their own graves at this point. Their story was pretty good, but even if I hadn't found the weapons, there was no reason for them to explore this far away from Jacksonhaven-central. Spies or civilians, they knew what would happen if they got caught, and now they have to face the consequences.

The Council has ordered me to "take care of it." It feels like some sort of test. They've already made it clear what they want my answer to be. I wanted to use the survey team as hostages. It seemed like the smarter decision, and it's what I thought would happen when I dragged them back to Belaforme—we have the son-in-law of their second-governor, for fuck's sake!

I don't think I really have a choice. The Council doesn't want hostages, they want supplies. Supplies we don't even need. Jacksonhaven wants their people back, but they're not willing to fork over the frankly ridiculous amount of raw resources we're demanding. Negotiations have fallen apart. The Council threatened Jacksonhaven's Triad of Governors, and now it's on me to make good on their promises.

This isn't what was supposed to happen, and now I'm as trapped as the survey. What I want is no longer of any concern. I know my duty, I know what I have to do. I have to teach our enemies a lesson.

I'm going to make the call later, when she's asleep. Finish the job myself.

The survey dies tonight.

With trembling hands, Amara checks the date. It matches the night Vinh left their bed at the retreat. The workglass slips through her fingers and clatters on the floor, realization opening her up like the very first cut of a dissection blade.

The assault makes sense now. Rival settlements raid one another all the time, but the level of destruction Jacksonhaven wreaked was abnormal. It was revenge, plain and simple. An eye for an eye, blood for blood. How could the Council have failed to consider the consequences of murdering the scientists? How could *Vinh* have failed to do so?

None of this makes any sense. There must've been a way to save the survey's lives, some way to save their own colony. Amara knows Vinh's always had a cold side, but she doesn't understand how her sweet wife could've fallen asleep after meting out an execution, enemies or not.

Or maybe she doesn't know Vinh as well as she thought.

017

The runaway crouches high in a tree, her hands and feet gripping the slender branches. She presses herself close to the trunk, her large eyes wide and watching. Her chest rises and falls in a rapid staccato. She's hiding.

But there's no hiding from what's hunting her now.

Not forever.

She knows it's close. She can hear it, sliding along the leaf-strewn ground, trickling up the bark of nearby trees. It'll be upon her in minutes. But there's nowhere to run, and she's so very tired. She sees the truth for what it is: The hunter will not tire. It will not stop, and it will not slow, until it has her. So she looks up at the moons she never called hers, and the stars she never got the chance to study. She thought she'd have more time. Silver light spills down through the dark leaves, caressing her face. It feels like a farewell.

And below . . .

It's been so long since It tasted blood . . . especially that from another world. Too long, perhaps.

It feels good, to get back into old habits. It feels good, to remember.

016

"Huh, that's odd."

Toyin, one of her new assistants, scoots closer from where they're perched on a hillside. They're a biochemist who defended their master's thesis not two days ago, but they're already her favorite. Except for one little thing. "Dr. Obi?"

"I'm sorry, who's that?"

"Sorry, Dr.—" Toyin gives a pained little smile. "Amara."

"Better." She forces a smile of her own. Dr. Obi is, or maybe was, her first-ìyá. (The life-extending technology at her family's disposal is formidable, but she left Great Ọ̀yọ́ a hundred or so standard years ago.) She hands them her trusty binoculars, gifted to her the day she passed her own defense. "Tell me what you see."

The world is alive and alight. The sun is shining, the bird-analogues are singing, the miscellaneous pollinators are buzzing. And down in the valley below, a pack of sixeyes is creeping through the grass toward a herd of arrowheads. Toyin informs her of as much.

Amara shakes her head, tutting. "No, *look*. Really look."

She knows Toyin's expertise deals with life on a much, much smaller scale: Their specialty is studying metabolisms via biomarkers. They spend all day slicing up microbial membrane lipids and analyzing the carbon content of the fragments. Megafauna aren't really their thing. But everyone on Amara's team is going to develop an appreciation for all levels of life, and them's the rules.

She needed to get out of the house and the lab, anyway, and Toyin's decent company. Reviewing the mycologists' exhaustive updated catalog of potentially medicinal and/or edible fungus-class organisms is not science. At least, it's not the sort that made her fall in love with the natural worlds of the galaxy. *This* is. (All mushrooms are fascinating, anyway. What they can do for humans is the least interesting thing about them, in her correct opinion.)

Toyin's mouth twists in frustration. Then they're shifting forward on their stomach, twisting the focus and zooming in.

"The arrowheads aren't doing anything," they mutter. "They're just standing there. Looking at the forest." They glance up at her for confirmation.

"That's right," Amara says, beaming with the pride of any pleased teacher. Then her expression falters. "I don't know why, though."

Toyin lifts the binoculars again. "They're not grazing, even. Do they know the sixeyes are there?"

"No," Amara says, absently. "If they did, the matriarch would've started the group warning call by now."

Toyin huffs. "Maybe they've just been drinking too much Gray lately."

Amara makes herself laugh a bit. "Maybe. But that's enough sightseeing for today." She stands, turns away. "Help me pack up."

Henry calls Amara a few hours after she gets home from work. If Amara had stopped to check the name on her talkglass, she wouldn't have answered. She'd been expecting

Vinh. She narrowly resists the urge to hang up, and continues braiding her hair for sleep.

"Hey, Amara," he says, and she can't tell if she's imagining the pitying smirk on his round face. "I just wanted to check in on you. Vinh told me you two had a spat?"

Amara grits her teeth. Vinh talked to *Henry* about *them*? That Vinh shared their secrets with her official new husband feels like a violation, a betrayal. Her melancholia quickly crystallizes into rage, white-hot and blade-sharp. She hisses as her fingers tangle, painfully, in her hair.

Honestly, the problem isn't even her. It's him. She can share. If Vinh wanted *Jesse*, and Jesse was fine with it all, Amara doesn't think she would care overmuch. Really. As long as she got to—

That's about where she cuts off that train of thought. She doesn't want to analyze the part of her that wonders about such things.

"It's none of your business," she grinds out, slowly freeing her fingers from the ruined braid and starting over.

"You're right, it isn't," he replies after a long moment, surprising her. "It's just that Vinh says you're angry at her, and she's really broken up about it."

She should have told me *that. She shouldn't have gone to him.* "I'm not angry at *her*, Henry."

"Oh." He lets out what sounds like a happy sigh of relief. "Oh, good. Is it just that time of the month?"

Amara starts to imagine all the ways he could disappear. She could probably make it look like an accident. She might even be able to get Jesse to help. "No."

"Huh, okay." Another painfully long pause. "I know we started off on the wrong foot, but I just want her to be happy. This whole thing is awful, but we both have to work together to make that happen. Truce?"

Amara ties off the braid with a silk ribbon. If she tells him to fuck off, he'll just squeal to Vinh. "Fine."

"Great. Excellent. Have a good night, Amara."

She hangs up. Then she leaps to her feet, yanks back her arm, and flings the talkglass. It doesn't shatter, as she'd hoped, but merely bounces off the window and lands on the floor with a thump.

Amara stands there, in the middle of Jesse's bedroom, and lets out a short little scream. Faintly, she hears the front door shut as Jesse leaves the house.

015

*T*hump.
    Thump.
  Thump.

Jesse awakens. There's someone making their way down the hall toward him. Something, maybe.

Thump.

Thump. Thump.

Getting faster, now. Of course, it's Amara, sleepwalking.

Thump-thump-thump.

But Amara doesn't sleepwalk, and the beat of footfalls against the flooring is too heavy to be her. And something else is off. Too many feet, maybe. Too many legs. Jesse peels back the covers and sits up.

Thumpthumpthumpthumpthump.

Well, then. Better to go and see what it is than lie on the couch and let it come to him first. The second his bare feet hit the floor, the footsteps stop. That's when he realizes, in the absence of that awful pattern. Not footsteps at all. It was knocking, but not at the door. From below. Under the house.

Jesse stands, as if pulled by innumerable, invisible hands. And then . . . his eyelids slide halfway down. His heart rate slows. Whatever parts of him that were truly awake, if any, fall suddenly asleep. In the cavity that consciousness leaves behind is a song. A low, droning moan, spreading out from him and echoing back in every direction. It is a call, a sum-mons, a serenade.

Amara might be upstairs, fast asleep in bed, but she's a light sleeper. *Quietly, quietly.* Jesse walks from the living room to the back door. *Quietly, quietly.* No need for shoes.

And then he's out, he's free. He knows this path better than he knows himself. One foot in front of the other, step by step. Repeat. He's there. At the pool's edge. On his knees before the Gray. The supplicant before the altar.

There's a smooth sheen to the pool, the glisten of fresh scar tissue. It ripples.

Air catches in Jesse's throat, and then—something unfurls, deep within the Gray. The pool explodes into color. Stripes of iridescent teal and orange flutter across the surface. Purple veins spiral and dance to the pitter-patter of his pulse. The rainforest dulls in the face of such beauty. Throbbing tendrils inch forward from the edge, liquid and leechlike.

Jesse's mouth fills with saliva as a lustrous filament nears his knee. And yet . . . "Not like that," he hears himself say. "Not . . . that."

The Gray listens. It recedes. It stills. Jesse crawls forward, mesmerized. All he can see now is his reflection. Except he's perfect. Poreless skin. A nose his aunt never broke beneath her fist. Lashes stuck together with Gray, glinting like ser-rated golden teeth. The lips pull, oh so slowly, into an el-egantly cruel smirk. A low sound comes from deep within the reflection's chest. It's the moaning he heard before. Just louder, closer.

Jesse can't stop himself. It wants him. He wants it back. His fingertips dip beneath the surface of the Gray. There's pressure, there, but only a little. Not enough to stop him from getting at the reflection. From getting at himself. A small electrical shock goes through him. He sucks in a breath; the pain is exquisite. The little hairs on his arms and on the back of his neck stand at attention. His pupils swallow the blue of his irises.

The reflection opens its eyes, bleeding red holes, something wet and legion writhing deep within.

Oh, the hunger, the hunger, the hunger.

Jesse's mouth flies open in a scream.

Jesse wakes up, snug as a bug on the couch. The covers are tucked in around him, so tight they're on the edge of smothering. That's how he likes it. That's how he went to sleep. Light slides in as the windows go transparent, trickling into his eyes.

He presses both hands, hard, to his face and drags them down. He turns onto his side, where there's a little rotating hologram of Amara and Vinh on the coffee table. Looking at their tiny smiling faces calms him down somewhat. But not enough. His heart is beating too loud and too fast.

He gets up from his makeshift bed and looks around at a room that is unrecognizably his own.

"Jesse?" Amara calls from down the hall. "Vinh's coming over for breakfast in five! That okay? Where's the pancake mix?"

Oh, fuck.

He stares at the door like it's some sort of beast about to pounce. He can't tell them. *Her* especially. He can't. He doesn't even know if what happened . . . happened. The uncertainty gnaws at him. The more he thinks about it, the more obvious the answer becomes.

Real, unreal, what does it matter? His friends can't help

him. They can't even help themselves. Jesse stumbles to the nearest bathroom, scrubbing the tears from his eyes. He turns on the faucet and splashes his face with cold water. It's good, the shock. He stares at the water in the sink. Nice, peaceful water. Normal water. A normal face staring back at him. He closes his eyes, considers the words lying heavy on his tongue.

"Above the stove, second cabinet on the left!" he calls.

"Already found it, but thanks!" Amara yells.

He jerks his head upward and grins at himself in the mirror until he feels what's on his face. Good, good. He's still got it. He heads up to Amara's room and grabs a fresh shirt from the closet. He pulls it over his head as he returns downstairs and walks, slowly and deliberately, into the kitchen. Vinh's already there, perched by the granite island and sipping a cappuccino.

There are huge dark circles under her eyes. She found out about what happened with Amara and Henry yesterday. Mostly because Jesse told her so she'd do something about it. And that something, apparently, is popping over for breakfast practically unannounced. All right, fine. They can play house. It's better than nothing. Better than silence and pretending that everything's hunky-dory, which are Vinh's usual responses to shit hitting the fan in her nonprofessional life. Covering one's nose and bringing up the fine weather doesn't make the mess go away. She stops saying whatever it is she's saying when she sees him. Her eyes go wide.

Amara turns around when Vinh goes quiet, and her lips pull into a grimace. "Woah, what's with that face?"

"Buddy, you okay?" asks Vinh, brows drawing together.

"Never better," says Jesse, and he makes himself stop smiling. He tucks stray strands of dripping hair behind his ears. "What about protein? How do we feel about tofu scramble?"

Amara and Vinh exchange a too-long glance as he grabs a pan, and he pretends not to see it.

014

The end begins with a chimpanzee.

At the height of its growth, when New Belaforme still had fabricators and was restricted only by the limits of human ingenuity, it was the size of a decent city. When Jacksonhaven's very first buildings were done, it was a little larger than the average Old Earth metropolis. No temporary mass housing, with three bunk beds per room. No cubicles virtually stacked on top of each other in their offices. A month after their own Landing Day, Jacksonhaven had its massive council chambers, its first library, and no less than three parks. They built a zoo; such was their excess.

Amara is out collecting fresh samples of Gray with Toyin when she finds the chimpanzee. They both wear full environmental protection gear, even though an individual flood of Gray is harmless to anything that it hasn't been specifically manufactured to eradicate—as far as they know, anyway. And so they're in reinforced hazmat suits, just in case.

They're about to start bagging vials when Toyin unfolds their wiry form from a squat, snaps shut their instrument tool-kit, and scampers over to Amara. "Dr. Obi? Ma'am?"

"I told you to call me Amara," she corrects sharply. Lately, she's had little patience, with herself or anyone else.

Toyin flinches behind the plastic film of their hazmat suit, their golden-brown eyes going comically round. Beads of sweat have already formed between their brows.

Amara sighs. "What is it?"

Toyin holds up a pair of tweezers. Between the pincers is a tiny chunk of gleaming white. "I must be wrong—I have to be wrong, but it looks like . . . It looks like . . . Well . . ." They lift an arm to scratch at their wiry black hair, forgetting that they're wearing a helmet. Their fingers slip off the top and they let out a mortified not-quite-laugh.

"Bone." Amara grips Toyin's arm, steadies it so she can get a better look. "A distal phalanx, or something similar." She breathes in and out, forcefully slow as she tries to fend off a sudden gut punch of panic. Her own hands shake now, so she lets them go. "The Gray . . . it's killing animals now." She drops back to the ground and packs up her samples. "Where exactly did you find this?"

"Just over there."

They lead her to the edge of a pearlescent tendril of Gray. When they take a step forward, Amara grabs their elbow and yanks them back. She points at a spot just above their heads. A couple meters away, the segment connects to a much larger Gray appendage, which in turn branches from the main body of the flood.

Toyin lets out a little gasp of horror. "How—That wasn't there when I left!"

Amara says nothing. Her world lurches to a spine-rattling stop. Toyin, crawling in the dirt around the edge of the flood site, wouldn't have seen it. Floating in the Gray, each bone gleaming deathly white, is a chimpanzee skeleton. It's completely intact, save for the distal phalanx of its right big toe. The poor animal must've escaped from Jacksonhaven's sprawling zoo; the skeleton has only just started to dissolve.

The slow but inexorable breakup of the collagen and calcium phosphate reminds Amara of a salt tablet in water.

"Please tell me you didn't touch the Gray, even with gloves," she grits out.

Toyin's voice is firm when they reply, "No, ma'am. Why?"

The tendril pulses.

"Did you see that?" Amara asks. Prickling sweat glues her gloves to her palms.

"See what?" asks Toyin.

"The Gray. It moved."

"I didn't see anything. Why would it move?"

As if in answer, the tendril squirms just a centimeter closer. The glittering tip swivels around along the dirt: a chiding finger, a wagging tongue. Searching, seeking.

Everything around them, down to the scuttling insects in the grass, holds its breath. Amara tries to swallow, but the spit sticks to her throat. She coughs violently, her whole body spasming. Toyin makes a tiny strangled sobbing noise as they come to the same realization.

When directly compared, the similarity between the chimpanzee and human genomes is 98.9 percent. The Gray may be near perfect in its precision, but it's not that perfect.

It's coming for them.

013

Amara tells Jesse immediately. They spend a day locked in his house. First, they try to convince each other that she's wrong. They fail. Then they try to figure out what the hell they're going to say to the Council.

The Council reacts as expected. Amara and Jesse are sworn to secrecy. There's no need to cause a panic while they whip up a miracle solution to save the settlement. The two of them are also excused, indefinitely, from participating in the settlement's reproductive program. Their time and energy would, of course, be better spent trying to keep their new home planet from dissolving everyone down to their constituent molecules. Amara and Jesse are thereby saved from their predicament by one far worse.

But they won't know how bad it is until they start running tests. They get dressed in full protective gear and prepare the samples from the chimpanzee site. Tendrils cut from a main flow don't actively seek out targets, but they're not taking their chances. From the field to the containment chamber, they handle the vials like grenades.

Toyin joins them soon after. Jesse's eyes narrow when he sees them coming in through the door, but he holds his tongue. They can't do everything alone, and her assistant knows the truth anyway. The Gray loses it when they drop in a tiny slice of human flesh. Shimmering filaments go at the muscle fibers and connective tissue like it's personal, ripping in like some rabid beast—

Amara stops herself, takes a deep breath. It's not alive. It's not sapient, or sentient, or even aware on the most basic level.

"We need to tell Jacksonhaven," Toyin whispers. They head toward the decontamination unit, to where their talkglass sits on a lab bench. "We need to warn them."

"Don't you dare," Jesse says, smiling as he strides to block them. "Not after what they did to us."

"We have to," Toyin says again. They're shaking a little. "They don't deserve to die like that poor animal."

Jesse tilts his head. "Why not? They brought this on themselves."

Yes, it's technically possible the chimpanzee was at fault, but they've never seen the planet launch an attack on a single loose organism before. When it comes down to it, the likelihood of Jacksonhaven damaging the environment more than this world could tolerate is far higher than that of a single chimp.

"Because they're people!"

Amara's brows shoot up. She's never heard Toyin raise their voice before. She's never heard them sound anything other than deferentially anxious.

"We'll have to agree to disagree," Jesse says. He's grinning so hard now his eyes are nearly squeezed shut. "You're not telling them anything. The Council gave us direct orders. We tell them what we find, no one else. Not our friends, not our families, and certainly not the assholes who put us in this situation to begin with." He puts a hand on Toyin's shoulder, so very near their neck. "Am I clear?"

"Jesse," Amara warns. She doesn't like the way her friend's speaking to her assistant. Not at all.

Jesse looks her in the eye, still smiling as his fingers tighten on Toyin. "Am I clear."

"Yes." Toyin wrenches themself away. "We're clear."

"Good!" says Jesse. "Let's get back to work."

012

Of course, Amara isn't surprised when Toyin comes in the next morning, minutes before Jesse arrives, and gives her a desperate look that tells her everything she needs to know. She feels pride—and fear. She doesn't know what the Council is going to do when they find out. And of course, there's Jesse.

As it turns out, nothing happens, at least where their elected leaders are concerned. The Council, apparently, has been keeping tabs on Jacksonhaven for the past forty-eight hours, and they've been getting only static back on all channels. The enemy settlement has always kept its communications private, and so have they. Auditory arms races are a time-honored tradition for rival colonies; everyone dedicates a disgusting amount of resources to bolstering their own lines' security, while inventing new ways to listen in on the enemy. It's an evolution of sorts. But closed channels spit utter silence. Not static. Something's broken.

There's no response to Toyin's warning, either. The Council has Amara and Jesse send out some of the colony's precious spydrones that night. When Toyin moves to join them in the control room to help keep an eye on the video feeds, Jesse slams the door in their face. Amara breathes out a sigh of relief; she's just grateful that's all Jesse's doing in response to Toyin's betrayal.

Everything looks normal for the first six hours, as the drones fly toward the other side of the continent. Lush, vibrant rainforest, zipping by in a brilliant blur. Then dense jungle thinning out into scattered leafy patches, and then finally rolling grassland.

At six hours, fifty-seven minutes, and twenty-three seconds, they lose everything. The visuals flash white before going dark. The audio waveforms drop flat. It all happens instantaneously, simultaneously. Amara and Jesse are left staring into black mirrors.

"So what now?" she whispers.

"You know what," Jessie replies.

Maybe Jacksonhaven caught the spydrones. Maybe they're taking them apart right now, recycling the material for tools to use against New Belaforme. Maybe they just destroyed them. Or maybe something else did.

Whatever happened, there's nothing for it. They have to go see for themselves. Amara and Jesse take off in a helicraft immediately. Along the way, they'll gather as much information as possible about the coming Gray eruptions. And there must be further eruptions on the horizon. The flow that killed the chimpanzee was hundreds of kilometers away from either settlement; the planet may not be sentient, but it isn't stupid. It doesn't waste resources. That means it's going to try to purge itself of all human life, not just Jacksonhaven. Yes, *purge*. Somehow, the term *self-cleansing* no longer feels right.

Based on their previous observations of the Gray's pattern of attack, Amara and Jesse theorize the purge will begin in a circular formation around New Belaforme and Jacksonhaven before closing in. Their priority, after figuring out what happened to the enemy settlement, is to determine the circumference of the kill zone so their colony can relocate and decide next steps. Their third goal is to uncover what Jacksonhaven did to make the planet identify them as contaminants in the first place. Their fourth and final objective is to find out *when* the planet will begin murdering them all in earnest.

Amara directs the helicraft above a tide of emerald-green trees and pilots it east, toward Jacksonhaven. At first, the going is slow. The console lets out a few dutiful beeps when they cross the contested border into enemy territory, but there's nothing else to mark the rival settlement a dozen kilometers in. By now, Jacksonhaven's air defense should be lobbing warning shots—but there's nothing. Only the bland static of the radio, and the helicraft's scanners show no signs of incoming missiles. They do find the spydrones, though. The charred husks of them, anyway. They were shot down by camouflaged, automated ground turrets before they even got a hundred meters into Jacksonhaven territory. But the fact that no one's come to collect and dismantle them is . . . indicative.

A few low buildings start to pop up from the savannah below, one by one. Outposts.

"See anything?" Amara asks.

"Nothing the helicraft isn't already showing us," Jesse replies. He won't meet her eye. "You?"

"Same as you." Amara's grip on her security belt tightens. "Is something wrong?"

Jesse's hands still over the controls for a second, a minuscule flinch. This is followed by long, meaningful pause. "Guess."

The grasses below ripple in a single, vast wave, the wind ruffling the blades like a hand through hair.

Amara sighs. "Are you mad at me?"

"If I were mad at you, you'd know." He makes a slight

adjustment to the helicraft's trajectory. "But I think you knew Toyin was going to do what they did. You should've told me. Or stopped them yourself."

"They're just trying to help everyone survive, Jesse," Amara says. Toyin was right.

Jesse laughs. It's a real, belly-deep laugh, the kind that brings tears to one's eyes. "Amara, Jacksonhaven doomed us." He sounds so, so tired.

"It's not like we wouldn't have trashed their reproductive center, and worse, given half the chance," Amara insists. "Right now, it's humanity against this whole world. Polity lines and past grievances don't matter anymore."

"And suddenly she's a saint." Jesse shakes his head in disbelief. "Where's that magnanimity when—"

"Henry's completely different. It's only right that—"

"I didn't say anything about him," Jesse says slowly. His shoulders have risen by a few centimeters. "Don't put words in my mouth."

She doesn't really hear him. "You just don't get it, do you? You've never lost anyone like I have."

Jesse turns to look at her fully. His grin is a white-toothed gash. "Oh, fuck you."

"I'm sure you wish someone would."

There it is: a line crossed. He freezes, the smile evaporating. It's hardly the worst thing she's ever said to him. But she said it with the explicit intention to wound—and that's what struck him.

"I'm sorry." How did they get here? "I didn't mean it. I don't know why I even said it. I know you don't . . . want that—"

"It's fine," he says. It's not. The corners of his lips twitch; he's attempting another smile. "Look, I . . ."

Jesse's attention snaps to the viewscreen. Dark clumps of

detritus are popping up from the grass, scattered around the few structures like breadcrumbs. Amara asks the helicraft's AI to identify the objects, even as Jesse zooms in. They're suitcases and satchels, primarily. There are a few ground vehicles too, some with their doors already flung open. It's as if everyone living on colony's fringe fled. The only thing missing is . . . everyone. There isn't a single person in sight. Unease closes Amara's throat. She can see the same thing happening to Jesse, the nervous crease between his eyebrows deepening into a canyon.

When they reach the main settlement, the sun peeks over the craggy horizon. The sensor readout is clear: no movement, no audio signal, not even at the very heart of the colony. They must've shut down communications themselves. Amara's breath quickens, unease swelling into horror as Jacksonhaven comes into view. If their scientists came to the same realization she did, it would make sense that the people would want to consolidate and hunker down behind their defenses.

The capital is as pristinely abandoned as its outposts.

The three-hundred-meter walls stand strong and proud and unscarred. As do the council chambers and the two libraries, gleaming white under the sun. Goldbeaks flit over the three sprawling parks alongside giant buzzing insects. A pride of lions nap within their painted enclosure at the center of the zoo. But there's no sign of humans.

Jesse makes a sound. Partly a whisper, partly a gasp.

"Oh," says Amara. "Oh no."

Death has come for Jacksonhaven. In every sense that matters, the main colony is gone. Half of the settlement remains flooded with Gray, as if a rippling iridescent shroud was thrown over the metropolis. Tiny dark specks float in the flood. Amara has Jesse take over the controls and whips out her binoculars, even though she already knows what she's looking at. Enlarged, the specks become humans, dissolving piece by painful piece. Miniature halos of crimson and ivory cloak every settler—a mist of blood pulled straight through the pores, swirled with dissolving yellow globs of fat.

Amara's eyes are stapled to the scene; she can't tear them away. The initial flood must have been massive, if it reached all the way to the outskirts and they're only seeing the dregs now.

The last of the Gray is already receding, leaving the buildings unscathed and the technology fully operational. The lions look happy enough, if a little damp. Even the food will be perfectly fine. They've already run all the experiments twice with Toyin. Jacksonhaven will be utterly devoid of human life. It already is, unless you're counting half-dissolved corpses in suspension.

With the entire settlement overtaken, their chances of unraveling the planet's reasons for killing them are between zero and none. But it doesn't really matter what the people of Jacksonhaven did to anger the world; they're dead. If there's anything Amara has learned from years of study, it's that when the Gray comes for something, there's no saving it. Their focus now needs to be on changing the planet's opinion before it strikes.

Jesse scans for human life signs anyway, though they both know the result the AI will offer. Amara numbly suggests scanning for missing transports, hoping that maybe someone, anyone, got away in time.

Yes, Jacksonhaven was New Belaforme's rival settlement, their sworn enemy. Yes, they raided New Belaforme a dozen times, essentially doomed them to failure and a tortuously slow death. Yet, Amara finds it surprisingly hard to hold on to her hate. These people died the worst death imaginable, without warning. Without a chance to say their final good-byes. But perhaps that was a small mercy.

Recent lab results suggest that being submerged in activated Gray would be significantly worse than being burned alive or dunked in acid or boiled in oil, because the Gray discriminates when it comes to digestion. Simulations and highly controlled experiments have revealed that it goes after nerve tissue last, even taking what appear to be extra measures to preserve the life of its prey until the brain is consumed. If a victim of the Gray has a central nervous system capable of registering physically harmful stimuli, then it feels everything up until the very end. Amara wonders if the half-dissolved people down there are conscious of anything beyond their own suffering. Are they aware of the helicraft hovering overhead? Do they know they're being watched? Pitied?

There's a flicker of movement at the edge of her field of view. Amara turns slightly in her seat to get a better look. One of the bodies is turning, pushed by the flow of Gray. She zooms in, and suddenly a face fills her vision. Pale, serrated flesh. A swollen tongue sagging out of a screaming mouth, like a plump grub peeking from its burrow. Shimmer-slick eyes bulging out of their sockets. Another nearly imperceptible movement. Something floating in the matrix just bumped into the corpse. Another twitch. What is it?

"What do you see?" Jesse asks.

"I don't know. Give me a moment. . . ."

Amara's shaking fingers slip on the focus twice before her view expands. There's nothing around the corpse. It's not a corpse at all.

It's alive.

And it's screaming, and convulsing, thrashing, and, and . . . and then it just . . .

Bursts.

Shredded scraps of skin flutter in the Gray like flags in the breeze.

The binoculars hit the floor with a clang. Amara's hands sink into her hair, fingers tugging thick strands right out of her skull. She swings back and forth on her seat, too fast to really calm herself. As if rocking is going to do anything. As if it's going to erase what just happened. She does this for a time anyway, until she can see anything besides blood exploding outward from every orifice.

"If you could stop now, that would be great," Jesse says pleasantly, and that's when she realizes she's still screaming. "You're going to asphyxiate yourself. What did you see?"

She turns to face him, breathing hard. He's giving her a contemplative look, his brows drawn up in thoughtful sympathy. He's so calm, so controlled. Everything she could never be. But then again, he didn't see what she just saw.

"Someone. They were still alive," she croaks. "The Gray got inside and popped them like a fucking balloon. Just like that."

They've never seen anything like that before. It was like the Gray was taunting her.

"Don't worry." Jesse's voice is no longer so even. "We're going to—"

"What am I going to tell Vinh?"

"Really?" His expression doesn't change, but his eyes go cold. "She's *your* wife. What we need to do now is figure out how to break the news to the Council."

"Preventing this was my job. The whole fucking point of me." Amara lets out a broken little moan.

Jesse closes his eyes for a handful of seconds. "This wasn't your doing, Amara. The only ones at fault for this are Jacksonhaven's people."

Amara looks into his eyes. Unshed tears blur her vision. "But do you think she'll blame me, still?"

"Is Vinh's opinion of you really your top priority at the moment?" he asks, so very slowly. Every word is measured out, gram by gram onto the fragile scale between them. "There's nothing, no one else to worry about?"

He clearly desires a response, but Amara doesn't really have anything to say to that, so she falls back into her seat and twists open her water bottle. Jesse turns the helicraft around as she chokes down deep, desperate gulps. He keeps sneaking curious, narrow-eyed glances at her, gaze flickering from the Gray to her and back again, but Amara pretends not to notice. Jesse is Jesse.

They circle the sunken city two times before they admit to themselves they have to go back and report. There's no avoiding the inevitable, a truism that sinks its razor-sharp teeth into Amara as the helicraft pulls up. The light of morning sets the Gray afire, making the opalescent surface twinkle in waves. It's as if the flood is fluttering its fingers at them, waving goodbye! For now! And as they lift into the air, dawn illuminates what they missed on the way to their enemy.

The helicraft is set to pick up the barest whisper on any frequency. Now it finally latches on to a signal, the last message sent out from the city on repeat from a personal device:

"It's coming . . . Help me . . . Please, it's coming. Someone . . . It's here, oh Saints, it's here . . ."

Jacksonhaven fell prey to hubris. Their colossal, useless walls stand as testament. Amara can only imagine the resources it took to build them, the level of deforestation required and the resulting habitat disruption. Under the shimmer of Gray, tiny magnetic tracks stretch out like the plasmodiocarp of a slime mold from the back of the city, a vast web of uncaring avarice. They went too far. They thought they could sink their fangs into the planet without it noticing. And with their fall, Jacksonhaven doomed every human on the planet. Amara thought she knew fear before, when she saw that body. That fright is nothing under the weight of the terror that consumes her now. She is drowning within herself.

Every hollow, all the way to the horizon, is swollen with Gray, massive rocky boils about to burst. The planet won't be wiping out a targeted area.

It will purge the entire surface.

011

S ay I'm wrong," Amara yells. "Say I'm wrong, *one . . . more . . . time.*"

"I'm not saying you're wrong!" Vinh says. "I'm saying you can't be certain, not yet—"

Something fragile and expensive explodes against the wall.

Neither of them are the type to get violent during a fight. He knows that. He *knows* that. Likely one of them just forgot their surroundings and knocked something over. But the sound—it brings back things he drowned in the half-frozen sludge of a lake on Etretat II.

Jesse feels the planet purr beneath his feet.

He can't take it anymore.

He flees.

J esse falls to his knees before the pool. "Please. Please. Stop this."

A ripple passes over the Gray.

"What the fuck does that mean?" he snarls.

A pause; a held breath. Then the pool flashes cinnabar-red. Coal-black. Gold-yellow.

"I didn't ask for this!" The scream tears itself from his throat. "This wasn't what I wanted!"

All he wanted, all he has ever wanted, was to keep them. It's for the worst. The three of them—they were never meant to be. But he can't let them go. He needs them as much as they need each other.

"I don't want to lose them," he whispers. His fingers, mere centimeters away from the pool's glistening edge, curl into fists. "Don't let me lose them."

A tendril snakes up from the edge of the pool, and Jesse flings himself backward before it can make contact. His mind returns to him then in a shriek of shock. What was he thinking? What happened that night was only a dream. It didn't mean anything, up to and including that the Gray actually . . . what? *Cares* for him? He laughs, bitter and brittle. He is pathetic.

The Gray slides back, as if in acquiescence. It should be impossible; once it has a target, it does not, cannot stop. And yet. Jesse drags himself upright, breathing hard. He heads back to the settlement, thinking of nothing. Nothing, save for the fact that for one horrible moment, he wanted to reach out too.

010

There has to be a solution, some way to stop the Gray or avoid it, despite everything Amara has gleaned from her work. She is keenly aware of the fact that needing something doesn't necessitate its existence, but that's not going to stop her and Jesse from doing everything they can to rescue the settlement. She has to save Vinh.

They figure out pretty quickly that hiding from the Gray is as impossible as they feared. The sludge seeps through dirt and stone, metal and plastic. It can slither up vertical inclines. No mix of burning, freezing, or chemical treatments slows it down. Amara's family owns a dozen or so floating settlements, but with all the fabricators onworld under meters of Gray, there's no way New Belaforme would be able to cobble together any sort of flight-capable station. Helicrafts run on solar-powered batteries and can theoretically remain airborne forever, but there's just not enough space for food to feed even a handful of colonists until the Gray recedes. They'd never be able to touch down to grab more resources, anyway; the Gray "remembers," and they could never risk contamination. There is no hope of rescue. No ship from the Primacy is coming to save them.

They requisition all the probes, rovers, and drones they haven't already commandeered and scour the planet's surface for any crack or crevice that might remain untouched. They get the answer they feared.

One night, Amara finds herself in Jesse's sector rather than the other way around. He's normally better at work-life balance; he's typically out of his lab and in hers before dinnertime.

It always strikes her how bare he keeps his space. It goes beyond neatness. He never lets himself settle in. If or when they evacuate, not that there'd be a point, he'll be the first out the door. The bookshelf behind his desk has only the essentials: his trusty lab journals, some cheap but treasured keepsakes. All of his notes are backed up on his workglass, and he keeps his favorite rocks in a glass case under the bed she sleeps in.

There are only two images on the walls. Both are holograms, offering vivid three-dimensional views and multiple shimmering interfaces for interaction. One is a poster displaying the geological timescale of Etretat II across four colorful ladders of labels. The other is a picture of Amara and Vinh. Jesse dragged them on a hike to the top of a mountain, once, and here's the proof. Simpler times.

He's staring at something in his hands. "Ninety-three million years ago," he says quietly, "the oceans of this world were dominated by this creature and its cousins. Hold out your hands."

Amara does, and he presses a small, smooth fossil into her waiting palms. The body is split into three distinct sections, each separated into fine segments. At one end is a conical, helmetlike structure she assumes must be the head. There are ten little divots on top, ostensibly where eyes once were. "And now?"

"You know, one of the first things we noticed about this world were the mass extinctions," Jesse says. "At several points in the fossil record, we see vast numbers of species, and members of each species, preserved en masse in lower, older strata. Group vanishing acts in the next, younger layers up. Barely any time at all, geologically speaking, between them. But most colonized worlds show evidence of at least a few global die-offs." He looks at her. "Do you know what the conservative cutoff for a mass extinction is?"

He's a good teacher. She turns the fossil over and over in her hands. "Seventy-five percent of species lost in two million years or less."

He nods, his gaze distant. "We've gone back, reviewed work we thought was incomplete or shoddy. In the post-extinction strata we've reexamined so far, we see nothing. *Nothing* but coccoids, filaments, rods in chert. Toyin and their buddies found some putative tetracyclic sterols, but mostly it's just microfossils and the occasional giant stromatolite field. It looks like the damn early Mesoproterozoic. . . . Amara, the planet completely sterilized itself of virtually all multicellular eukaryotic life *three* times over its history. At least. We . . . *I* could be wrong, there's always bias, but . . ."

"I thought the Gray was meant to protect life."

"Protection can mean many things. Maybe it was protecting itself. Maybe it was protecting its life from something worse than death by disassembly." He shakes his head. "Two hundred and fifty-two million years ago on Earth, at the end of the Permian Period, volcanic eruptions raised global temperatures and acidified the oceans. Eighty to ninety-six percent of all species, gone." His eyes drift closed. "What's happened here makes the Great Dying, as it is called, look amateurish."

Their only hope is to somehow get back in the planet's good graces. With the help of New Belaforme's general AI, Amara and Jesse figure out where the most active hollow is and jump into a helicraft. Swaddled in full protection gear, and then some—not that it'll do anything but slow them down if the hollow decides to explode—they set up their equipment and begin running tests.

Initial scans indicate that this hollow is the oldest on-world. Subsurface structures connect it to twenty hollows nearby; the map they've been building suggests it's linked to every Gray-spewing pit in a massive planet-wide network. If they have any chance of digging up the secret to surviving, it's here. Amara's team has been searching for the center of the planet's deadly web ever since they discovered the Gray—she doesn't know whether to curse the gods she doesn't quite believe in for obstructing their path, or to thank them for finally bestowing this discovery.

"I'm going to get a closer look," Jesse says.

Amara doesn't look up from where she hacks chunks of rock out of the hollow's side. "Send a drone."

She picks up a fragment and examines it. There's something odd about it. She knows from Jesse's initial reports that hollows are mostly composed of uplifted sedimentary rock, formed under relatively low pressures and temperatures as continental plates collide. But throughout this piece's structure, there are vesicles—tiny holes that could've only been formed by gas bubbles trapped in lava. What she's seeing should be impossible; hollows aren't volcanoes, though their explosions are similarly destructive. It's the first sample she's seen like this.

It's a good thing she has an expert with her.

"Does this look igneous to you?" she asks as she starts hammering out another piece of rock.

Jesse doesn't respond. She stands and finds him kneeling about two meters away from the edge of the hollow's crater. A chill skitters down her spine, insectile and lightning quick.

The threat of an agonizing death hasn't tampered his rashness in the slightest.

"Get down from there and look at this!" Amara calls sharply, waving a sizable lump of rock like bait.

He doesn't answer, doesn't turn around. Probably can't hear her. She activates the two-way communication system built into her hazmat suit.

"Get down here before you fall in!" she warns him. Coldness presses its palm against the back of her neck, taps its frozen fingers along the base of her skull.

Something's off. The foreboding twist of her gut is all intuition, that of prey caught in the eyeline of a hidden predator. All she knows for certain is that something is terribly, horribly wrong.

"*Jesse*," Amara repeats, harsher now. Desperate.

"You have to see this," Jesse whispers, paying her no mind as he crawls closer. He sounds out of breath, but not as if he's been running. No, it's as if he's been punched in the gut. "It's—"

The hollow rumbles, a giant rolling its shoulders before it wakes. Where Amara stands, about a third of the way down from the crater, she merely stumbles. Jesse, crouched down at the very edge, is flung violently forward.

Amara hears his strangled scream as the rock under his feet crumbles into dust. She scrambles to the top of the hollow, terror roaring through her veins. Her lungs burn as though filled with acid.

No, please, no, not Jesse—

Amara has never offered an earnest prayer in her life but now she begs with every atom of her being. *Please, please, please.*

By the time she reaches the edge, there's only air.

Her best friend. Her confidant and companion. Her

partner in crime and in the laboratory and in so much of her life—

Gone.

There's only Gray, gorged on life, gorged on *Jesse,* on the man it sucked down its toothless, bloody, shimmering throat.

Amara stands there for a moment, trembling. Then her body gives out, and she gives up all hope. She crashes to her knees, stomach acid filling her mouth in a sour torrent. She is a jagged chunk of wreckage slammed against unforgiving rock, splintering and sodden, shoved out to sea, completely and utterly adrift.

Jesse.

Jesse.

Oh, Jesse.

Amara squeezes her eyes shut to stem the hot tide of tears, but in the end her efforts are just as inconsequential as her prayers. The world blurs around her. This is her doing. She didn't love him enough.

If she had, she would have caught him in time.

009

A fist smashes into Vinh's office door, followed by what sounds like a boot. A sharp *"Shit!"* followed by a pained groan.

Amara.

Vinh commands the door to open.

Her wife stands there, still halfway in her protective gear, trembling violently. Mascara streaks down her face like war paint.

"He's dead," Amara sobs.

The words bounce off Vinh like a rubber ball on concrete. "What?"

Amara stumbles inside. "He's dead." In the small space, her whisper sounds impossibly loud.

The floor lurches beneath Vinh's chair, as though the tiles have been turned to sludge. She couldn't make herself stand, even if she wanted to. "Jesse?"

Amara nods once, slumping against the wall.

"No," Vinh says, firm. Unyielding. Yes, good. At least her voice projects some semblance of the self-control she's never really had. "No, that's not possible."

"I saw him fall into the hollow, Vinh. I *saw—*"

A broken, sawed-off laugh scrambles up Vinh's throat. It emerges as something close to a sob. "You must be—"

"You finish that sentence, you tell me I *must be mistaken,*

I'll go ballistic," Amara says thinly. "*I* was there. *I* was with him. You weren't!" Her jaw flexes. "Where were you?"

Vinh's eyes flash. The accusatory note in Amara's voice was no accident. "I was here, in my office, doing what I could to keep this colony safe—"

"No. I don't mean *today*. I mean for a long while. Something in Jesse changed. He needed us, he needed help, and I couldn't do it all alone." Her voice lowers. "Where were you?"

She is being so fucking unfair.

"What do you want me to say, Amara?" Vinh asks. "That this is my fault? Jesse is—was Jesse. He's always been just out of reach."

"No, no. That's not true. Honey," Amara spits out, stalking closer, "he *changed*. Something in him shifted. But it's not as if you'd know, would you? We never saw you. You barely came over, barely spoke. Too busy with your husband."

Suddenly, Vinh is standing. Their faces are only centimeters apart. "And how would *you* know?" she hears herself say. "You drive everyone away."

Amara laughs. "No, Vinh, that's your move. If anything, I pull too hard."

"Yes." Vinh bares her teeth. "Yes, maybe that's true. That's why no one can stand to be around you. Do you have any idea how exhausting it is? All the criticism and cajoling and the *infinite* condescension?"

"At least I care," Amara says, oh so quiet. "You abandoned us both."

That's it. At that moment something awakens within Vinh, a thing with too many eyes and too many teeth. It's always been inside her, but she's never let it get at her wife before. She's allowed it to stir the water, and even come up for air once or twice, but never this.

"Well I'm sorry, baby." Vinh leans in, close enough to

kiss. She lets her gaze fall to her wife's lips. "But you made it real fucking easy."

Amara twists on her heel.

Vinh watches her go. She can't even bring herself to call Amara back. With the press of a finger against a screen, she locks the door. Then, only then, does she let the tears fall. She slumps over her desk, her face dropping into clawed hands. Blunt nails dig into her temple, her cheeks.

A sudden, all-consuming cold floods Vinh's veins, freezing her from the inside out despite the thick, smothering fug of almost-afternoon. She feels like she'd shatter at the slightest tap. A small, keening noise that could be a growing scream traps itself in her mouth and sinks into her tongue, along with her teeth. She's all right. She's going to be all right; it's just that her body strongly disagrees. She shoves back into her office chair and cradles herself.

Jesse.

Her only friend.

And now he's gone, forever.

008

Amara has little time to mourn, given the circumstances, but it's no matter. She doesn't see herself returning to work after the half-hour-long, slipshod funeral. New Belaforme took her wife, and the planet took her best friend. Amara knew Jesse for every moment of her life that mattered. If a life is measured by the people who build it together, what does that make hers? What does that make *her*? Whenever she catches a glimpse of her reflection, be it in a storefront window or a puddle in the road, she finds herself shivering. Oh, it's not that she doesn't recognize herself, the red-eyed, sunken-cheeked woman staring back at her. It's not that she doesn't know what she's capable of now.

She berates herself for her stupid dreams, for every childish plan she spun in her head for the three of them. Ever since Jesse convinced her to take Vinh back that day on Etretat II, she harbored a fantasy of building a comfortable little life in some faraway alien paradise. But whenever she imagined her future with Vinh, Jesse was there too. Instead of a family, she is alone. Instead of the dream, she has this nightmare—all her hopes and wishes reflected in dark blood and shimmering Gray. There is nothing left to live for except herself. It's enough, but only just.

Amara didn't want to have a funeral reception. She didn't want to field questions about Jesse's disappearance; the official story is that he was mauled by some unseen beast, hence the closed casket. She didn't want to listen to Councilwoman Margaret give her meaningless, insultingly brief speech. She didn't want people she feels nothing for in Jesse's house, looking at their things and trying to console her. But here she is, her lungs burning with funerary incense.

Someone touches her elbow. Amara doesn't even bother turning around. They're just another intruder. She imagines their features instead: brows curved with pity she doesn't want, eyes swimming with unshed tears. Every face a shallow simulacrum of sympathy, lips still dusted with crumbs of her dwindling food rations. Not that it matters.

"I'm sorry for your loss."

Amara jerks as if from an electrical shock. It's Henry. He's in her house because Vinh brought him. He's talking to her, *touching* her because Vinh brought him. Amara's vision flashes scarlet, deep and dark and cruel as the mist of gore surrounding a Gray-eaten corpse. She wrenches her arm away and just leaves, manually slamming the door behind her. She shuts herself in the office Jesse insisted was theirs.

A portrait hangs on the wall facing the desk, a solid picture of Jesse, Vinh, and Amara taken with an antique camera. There's even a hand-carved wooden frame and a sheet of glass over their smiling faces.

Amara drives her fist into it. Glass shatters and spills onto the floor. Blood wells up between her knuckles in thick, garnet-bright droplets.

Oh. She shouldn't have done that. She shouldn't have run. Henry's probably gloating about it, under his vacant smile. Amara's fingers curl tighter, squeezing out more blood. She has never genuinely wanted someone dead before, but she does now.

The door swings open. Vinh enters. They haven't spoken,

since . . . Amara hides her hand behind her back, not that it matters. The shards of glass clinging to the frame are flecked with crimson. Vinh makes a sad little sound as she pulls Amara's clenched hand out. When she moves in, Amara thinks it's to kiss her on the mouth, but Vinh's lips brush her cheek instead.

"Stay here," Vinh says. "I'm going to get a first aid kit."

She closes the door softly behind her.

As blood drips onto the floor, Amara watches the last loose shards of glass fall from the broken portrait.

Vinh never comes back.

007

Grieving or not, Amara still has a job to do, and it's expected she'll do it. That's fine; she's good at keeping up appearances if nothing else. After all, what else was her marriage with Vinh, besides a drawn-out lie? What little Amara managed to glean from the data she and Jesse gathered was that they have approximately four days left. The gargantuan hollow at the center of the Gray network will erupt, setting off a chain reaction that will ultimately bathe the entire planet in a death painstakingly designed for humanity.

Amara informs the Council, and they inform the settlement. There is surprisingly little rioting. Or perhaps the mere handful of brawls and burnings should've been expected. There's nothing anyone can do but make their peace and die. By now, her fear has crystallized into a strange sort of acceptance. Knowing death awaits makes her feel very wise, and very tired. There's a peculiar strain of contentment in such utter exhaustion.

Amara spends the first half of her last estimated ninety-six hours in the lab, all by herself. The others have gone home to their families, but she has neither a home nor a family. She and Vinh have made amends, and Vinh said she loved her. Even though she left Amara bleeding in Jesse's office. Even though Amara now finds herself alone, yet again, in a cold lab with half the lights off. She stares vacantly at a vat of Gray collected via drone from the chimpanzee site. She taps the wall of glass separating her from the sample with an unused writing stylus. There's nothing to calculate, nothing to work out.

She wonders whether her university advisors would be proud of the work she's done here, despite it all. She's one of the very few reasons this colony lasted as long as it did, but her research beyond the Gray and its systematic purging of unwanted life-forms was limited. Bounded by the practicalities of establishing a new colony. She wasn't exploring; she was sorting. She discovered numerous species each day, simply by being in the field and recording, but her job was restricted to broad descriptions and categorization: dangerous, not dangerous; useful, not useful; important, unimportant; interesting, uninteresting. The details she obsessed over in grad school were left for her staff and other scientists to puzzle out. For so long, what she did didn't feel like science. There was no passion in it, no wonder. No love either, outside of the scant moments she escaped into the field with Toyin and her binoculars. Not until the planet decided to kill them all and she dove into researching the Gray with Jesse.

A warm hand presses against her back.

"How'd you know I'd be here?" Amara asks. She knows it's a stupid question. Her voice is rough from disuse.

"You weren't home."

It's not Vinh's voice. Amara leaps out of her seat and wrenches herself around.

"Jesse." She doesn't drag him into a hug like she aches to. She doesn't trust herself. She presses a damp palm to her forehead. "Wonderful, I'm hallucinating."

Jesse laughs through his nose, a little puff of air. "No. I'm alive."

He pulls her into an embrace, holds her as close as Vinh

once did. Amara grips the back of his shirt, the same one he wore under the hazmat suit, and presses her face into his chest.

"Alive?" she whispers.

He nods, his chin brushing the top of her head. "Alive. And I've never felt better."

He feels solid, warm, real. He even smells exactly the way he always did, a mix of cheap hypoallergenic detergent and even cheaper deodorant. She hugs him tighter, despite the growing ache in her arms. Protocol would demand that he go through five rounds of decontamination before even breathing the same air as her. Protocol can go fuck itself. Against the odds, against *all* odds, Jesse is alive.

"How?" Amara chokes out.

"I don't know." He lets out a long, slow breath. "All I know is that I'm here, with you. And that the Gray doesn't hurt me."

She pulls back to get a better look at him. "Don't joke about that."

"How else could I have survived?" Jesse smiles.

But did he really? Amara's gaze sweeps over him once more. She's less reassured when her eyes meet his. She's not certain that the Jesse in front of her is the one who fell into the pit, and that qualm is digging into the small of her back like a knuckle. She can't put a finger on what, but something's just off. Something's changed, again. Maybe it's that there's a subtle new symmetry along the lines of his face, a minuscule perfection. Maybe it's that she can't help but feel he didn't have quite so many teeth before.

No harm in asking. (She hopes.) "Is it really you?"

"Hm?"

"Are you Jesse?"

If her unease insults him, he doesn't show it. In fact, he

smiles again, that crisp, diamond-exact slant of his lips. "Does it matter, as long as I'm yours?"

He turns and presses his palm to the ID panel in the glass separating them from the Gray sample. A segment of the barrier slides away. The decontamination unit scans him twice, and then the door to the containment chamber slides open.

"The planet didn't just spare me, Amara," he continues. "The Gray tore me apart, but then it . . . remade me. This world shaped me, *saved* me. And it's going to save you and Vinh too." He rolls up his sleeve.

Amara knocks a fist against the glass. "Jesse, don't."

Gray separated from the main flow is mechanically inert; it stays where it is, but it's just as lethal. Jesse shoves his arm into the sample, waits ten seconds, and pulls it out again. His arm is perfectly intact, his skin completely dry. He laughs, triumphant. Amara is reminded of the arrowhead herd she saw the day Vinh proposed.

Jesse goes through decontamination again, not that a thousand rounds of scans and fast-acting chemical sprays could neutralize the Gray if it clung to him.

"We have two days." He rolls down his sleeve. "But on time is late. We need to get moving, *now*. Where's Vinh?"

As clear as cut glass, Amara hears the unspoken question. *Why isn't she with you?*

"She's with Henry." Amara sounds exactly as bitter as she feels. "Who else knows about you?"

"No one." Then Jesse gives her a long, thoughtful look. "We should keep it that way."

006

"We have to tell them! If there's a chance we can save the colony, we have to take it."

Jesse sighs. "Do you remember what I told you after you said my homeworld was beautiful?"

"You . . ." She swallows hard. "You said it wasn't always."

"Etretat II is close to two other established colony worlds, so the Judgment ships come every other decade. Before we were able to make ourselves valuable, when it looked like Noble Francia was going to leave us to die, it was hard to make ends meet." His expression is softer and colder than freshly fallen powder. "There's a point at which overpopulation is just as damning as underpopulation. Parents would bury their kids alive in the snow to save supplies for the ships when they came to collect."

"Jesse . . ." She reaches out to take his hand in hers. His fingers are unnaturally still between hers.

"I know you know about the Jacksonhaven survey," he says.

Amara freezes. "How?"

Jesse ignores that. "I want you to know *I* told Vinh to execute them."

Her body screams to take a step back, to put space between them. She doesn't move. "How could you?"

"You know, I stopped by Jacksonhaven on my way back,"

says Jesse, as if discussing the weather. "What I found there . . . The Gray doesn't go after isolated gametes, or any other type of individual human cell. It's meant for species, right? It's designed to kill whole living organisms, not specific, individual components."

"So? I don't understand. . . ." Then it comes to her. "The gestation chambers—they'll still be functional?"

Jesse beams at her. "Yes. Eventually, the Gray will leave Jacksonhaven. In addition to every piece of tech onworld, we'll have all the genetic stores we could ever need. Including the samples they harvested from us before planetfall."

"What are you saying?" Amara asks, as if she doesn't know exactly what he means.

"I'm saying maybe we should start from scratch. We don't need the rest of New Belaforme to build a future here. We don't need anyone but us."

It's as she thought, but the words still hit her like a hammer. Amara sucks a sharp breath into her constricting lungs.

"This is a harsh planet, Amara. No one knows that better than the two of us. But our new world is merciful too. It wanted to cleanse itself utterly, perhaps even wipe the slate clean and let life arise anew. But while I was in the Gray, I proposed an alternative. I don't know why It listened, but It did." Jesse's mouth curves into something that's not quite a smile. "I had Vinh kill the survey team for the same reason my grandparents killed the child who would've been my uncle. I did it for the same reason we need to keep what happened to me a secret. Chaff must be winnowed from grain. Gangrenous tissue must be cut from healthy flesh. The colony must die, but we don't have to go with it. The planet has agreed to spare two others."

Amara's hands begin to shake. What he suggests is horrifying, and yet she feels no horror at his proposal. *That* is what scares her. She would feel revolted, perhaps, if not for Henry. Any plot that could potentially end in his removal is one she can wholeheartedly get onboard with.

"The planet is generous; Jacksonhaven just took too much, and caused too much harm," says Jesse. "The world will grant us all we need and more if you let it in. You just have to give yourself up. Willingly."

"That's all?"

"That's all. Give up and give in. And you'll live as you've never lived before."

She does not know this man. This is not her Jesse—

No. No, this *is* the real Jesse, the man who'd been beneath that pretty skin all this time, just waiting for the right moment to claw his way out from under the smiling mask.

And oh, Amara loves him, whatever he is.

"What do we need to do?"

005

To keep up appearances, Amara goes grocery shopping. Everyone stocks up on ingredients for their last meal, a grand communal feast that will take place in the central park the next day, just before the purge begins. A handful of people—a silver-haired woman hefting a pillow-sized sack of marshmallows, a man in green by the dairy section— shoot her narrow-eyed looks as she winds through the aisles. Her heartbeat picks up as she passes by, but none of them approach her. Despite all her self-flagellation, they know that what's about to happen is Jacksonhaven's fault, and the enemy already got their just deserts. Most of the New Belaforme colonists just want to be with their families before the end, not gang up on one hapless biologist. What would be the point? Failure was always a possibility.

Amara inspects a bottle of wine. Would chardonnay or Bordeaux go better with the euthanizing poison the toxicologist whipped up for them? It probably doesn't matter which she gets. Everything is free, the poison has no scent or taste, and she has no intention of attending the feast. She drops both bottles into her bag and makes her way to the exit.

"Hey, Amara!"

She turns around, slowly. "Henry."

If her curtness has any effect on him, he doesn't show it. "I'm making my grandfather's famous cobbler for the feast," he says loudly, before his voice drops to a conspiratorial whisper. "Don't worry, I'll save us a big slice for the trip."

The trip? What—

Then he winks.

He knows.

Which means Vinh told him. Which means Vinh wants him to live, wants him to be part of their new life. She didn't ask Amara or Jesse, because she knew they'd be against it. Was she planning on sneaking the bastard into the hollow while they were distracted? Was she going to give Amara's place to this parasitic worm of a man?

This is unacceptable. Amara has the capacity to indulge Vinh in many things, but Henry is not fucking one of them. Old habits die hard, and she's spent her time since Jesse's return fantasizing about their future. Specifically, their future without this man. She'll die before she gives that up.

Vinh was right when she said Henry wasn't so bad. There's nothing wrong with him, exactly. In another universe, Amara might've even befriended him. If, in that universe, Vinh left Amara and fell in love with Henry of her own free will. Then at least Amara would be able to force down her feelings and move on until she could face them. She could learn to be happy for the pair. (At least, that's what she tells herself.) But this is all the Council's doing; they ripped her out of Vinh's life and shoved Henry into the space she left behind. Loving someone sometimes means letting them go, but it never means letting them get torn from you.

Amara forces herself to smile. The half-healed cuts on her fist throb in time with her elevated heartbeat. "Did you get your hazmat suit?"

He blinks at her, slow and stupid. "No, was I supposed to?"

"I guess you didn't get Jesse's message. We ran some new tests—we can't come into any sort of contact with Gray except that in the main hollow." Amara sighs. "I'll take you to get fitted now."

Henry's eyebrows lift. "Would a suit really make a difference? I thought Gray can get through anything."

Amara nods. "Yes, but if some landed on you while in a full suit, you'd have just enough time to take everything off before it got to your skin." She crosses her arms, daring him to disagree.

"Oh, I see." Henry scratches at his new patchy beard. "Sorry for the trouble, then."

Amara smiles wider, all teeth. "It's nothing. I was headed to the lab anyway, and Vinh hasn't picked her suit up yet either."

Henry beams at her as they head out of the grocery. "Vinh always talks about how you're such a good friend."

Is she imagining the emphasis on the last word? She thinks not.

She's not going to regret this.

Not at all.

Between trying on each of the differently sized hazmat suits Amara hands him, Henry sips from a cool glass of tainted water.

Not poisoned, exactly. Tainted.

She could've used the toxicologist's cocktail and made her job even simpler than it already is, of course. But that would be painless. There's no pleasure in Henry dying an easy death, and even the most slow-acting and painful of poisons would be a merciful end compared to what she has planned. After all Amara has been through, after all the suffering and sacrifices while he played house with *her* wife, he deserves this.

He deserves everything.

Faking comradery up until Henry started drinking was simple, though not quite effortless. Cajoling a man whom she has less than no respect for put a deeply sour taste in her mouth. Dosing his drink with a colorless, scentless neurotoxin collected from one of the continent's semi-reptilian life-forms, however, was like breathing. The easiest thing she's ever done in her life.

Amara leans against the counter of a resin-laminated lab table. "How does that one feel?"

"Hmmm," Henry says noncommittally. He smacks his lips as he pulls on the suit's matching pair of gloves.

"Doesn't it fit?" Amara tilts her head at him expectantly.

She wants him to meet her stare. She wants to see the punishment for his presumption play out. He thought he could join them. He thought he could replace her. He thought he could have Vinh and live.

Amara feels like laughing, but she's not willing to ruin the surprise. She's never killed anyone before, and no self-respecting scientist would waste an opportunity like this one. She wants to observe as the light starts to fade from his eyes, to note the exact moment when the man before her becomes a hundred kilograms of unthinking meat.

"The water tastes a little metallic, all of a sudden," Henry says. He smacks again, louder this time.

"It's the extra electrolytes," Amara replies smoothly.

"Oh." He walks around experimentally, testing out the stretch and pull of the suit's fabric. "I never said it before, but I'm genuinely happy you and Vinh have each other. I have to admit that I have feelings for her, but I'm still happy for you two." He turns this way and that. "In my next life, I want to be with someone that loves me as much as Vinh loves you. Disobeying the Council for each other, conse-quences be damned—how brave!"

Amara takes a deep breath. The dry, filtered air of the lab scrapes her lungs. She wanted—*wants* him dead, and he's going to die. Even if Vinh truly never felt for him, Henry's words change nothing. *Nothing.* He was doomed the second the planet decided to purge itself. Even if they did take him with them, the Gray would not accept him.

This is catharsis, simple and glorious. This is revenge. This is closure, in every sense of the word. This is making sure Henry and Vinh never see each other again, no matter the true nature of their relationship.

Henry pulls off the helmet, takes a shallow swallow of sterile air. "Do you have anything looser around the chest? This feels really tight."

"Sure thing. I'll grab the next size."

He finally looks at her when she doesn't get up. He blinks wildly for a moment, as if she's going in and out of focus. He wobbles, nostrils flaring. "I can't feel my hands, Amara," he says, whisper-soft.

"I know."

Henry's arm swings out. Whether to attack her or to find purchase, Amara doesn't know. She doesn't much care. He misses both her body and the table, and crashes to the floor. She hears the sick pop of a knee dislocating.

Henry bares his teeth in a wretched, pathetic, pleading smile. "What did you do?" he begs.

"I'm killing you." She says it matter-of-factly. "The Gray will do the real work, though. The venom is only meant to paralyze you. You'll still feel. You'll still suffer."

She pulls out her talkglass and begins composing a mes-sage to her team. She informs them that no work will be permitted before the end. There is no cure, no solution, no escape. Their last few hours would be better spent with their loved ones than hunched over a microscope.

"Vinh will never forgive you."

"Only if she finds out, which is unlikely. By the time we return, even your bones will be gone. I know you didn't bother to tell her you were coming with me." Amara shrugs. "But let's say that she does somehow discover what happened here. She wouldn't be angry at me for forever. You're not so much of a loss."

With that, Amara turns on her heel and leaves Henry drooling on the floor.

004

Henry hasn't come home. He said he'd be back hours ago.

There's no point looking for him. Vinh knows he's dead, in the same way she knew Bác Huy had died long before her parents broke the news.

She doesn't know whether the majority of her anger is directed at Amara or at herself—some part of her always knew this would happen. Nothing and no one gets between her and her wife, and she *knew* Amara decided Henry was an obstacle from the very first day. She saw the look in her wife's eyes. She understood what it meant.

Just as Vinh understood that nothing would happen between Amara and Jesse. What would she have done, if their situations had been reversed, if her wife had been shoved into the arms of some fawning stranger? It doesn't matter—that's what she tells herself, just as the answer crystallizes in her mind.

But deep down, Vinh knows exactly what she would've done: the same thing Amara has.

At exactly midnight, Jesse comes up the stairs and opens the bedroom door. Footsteps sound across the hardwood. Amara is awake before his hand falls gently on her shoulder. She's always been a light sleeper, but she knows she heard him because he wanted her to. Jesse only makes noise when he wishes. He sits daintily on the edge of the mattress, looking more comfortable alone with her than he has in months. This is one of the few times they've been in his bedroom together since they were assigned to each other.

His irises glow yellow-white in the light of the moons, like a canine's. "Did you sleep well?"

He's different. There were only so many tests she could run on him in secret, in the little time they had. What she does know is that his resting heart rate is twenty beats per minute, dangerously low. He barely breathes; Amara counted sixty breaths in the space of an hour. Yet his reaction time is five times faster. His eyesight and hearing extend far past that of a normal human. His muscle strength is beyond anything she's ever seen.

For a single terrified moment, after he'd told her the plan and they'd gone back to the house, Amara wondered whether she could truly trust him. Jesse is still her best friend; she's happy to put her life in his hands, but Vinh's? Another question entirely. But they have no choice.

Leaving is so, so easy. Amara crawls out of bed, dresses quickly, and pulls their packed bags out from the closet. Jesse can breathe and walk through Gray as if it were air, and the compiled results of the trials she was able to run suggest that she and Vinh will be able to do the same. But if they can avoid returning to New Belaforme while the other settlers' bodies are being dissolved, then they will. They have enough supplies to sustain themselves for two weeks, by the end of which the Gray will have receded from the colony. Amara hasn't actually seen Jesse eat or drink yet, and he only laughed when she asked if he needed to. But better safe than sorry, and there's no such thing as being overprepared.

Amara and Jesse leave the house for the last time. She doesn't look back. It was never her home. The walls hold nothing for her but pain. Hell with Jesse was still hell. And after she thought she'd lost him forever . . . Well. The farther away they get, the better. They creep out of the cul-de-sac and head left, intending to take a shortcut across the park.

No sooner do they enter the grounds than a dark shape at the corner of Amara's vision starts waving. Her heart skips a beat.

It's not Vinh. It can't be. This isn't the meeting place. She twists toward Jesse, but he's gone. No . . . he's hiding. This doesn't feel like when he fell into the hollow. She doesn't know how she knows, but Jesse's still there. Somewhere.

Waiting.

The shape walks over, swathed in darkness. "Fancy meeting you here!"

Amara knows that voice. It's Kazimir, Toyin's husband and the best astronomer on the science team. The couple were allowed to remain together due to their "compatibility." (Shit, *Toyin*. She hasn't seen them since Jesse kicked them out. Oh, brave, kind, forgiving Toyin. Maybe Jesse will let her clone them, once this is all over.)

"Hey, how's it going?" Amara forces out, palms growing damp. She wants to smash her forehead against a wall.

"I'm okay." The sound that slips from Kazimir's throat is not quite laughter. "Well, as okay as I can be."

Amara freezes as he pulls something long and black from under his arm. She recognizes it a moment later: just a portable telescope.

"I never saw stars like the ones here before," Kazimir says, "even when I took that trip out to Hahnera. Thought I'd get one last hour in while Toyin's sleeping, before . . . y'know. Does that make me a shitty husband?" He coughs and smiles bashfully, but recovers quickly. "What brings you out so late? Or early, I guess."

"I just . . . needed air, I guess." Amara gnaws at the inside of her cheek until she tastes iron.

"Yes. I get it." He sniffs. "You know, for a moment there I thought I saw someone else. Almost looked like Jesse! Can you believe that?"

"I can."

Amara and Kazimir both whirl around. There's Jesse. He's just . . . there.

Kazimir's mouth falls open. "How . . . how . . ."

"This is unfortunate," Jesse says, quiet enough so that only Amara catches his words. Unlike hers, his voice is as calm as a sea before a storm.

"You died," Kazimir whispers. He's looking at Amara now. "You said he died! You saw him die!"

"Kazimir, you should probably just go now," she says stiffly. She's not going to beg.

She grabs Jesse's sleeve and tries to move forward, but tugging her friend is like trying to drag a boulder.

"We can't have any witnesses," Jesse murmurs.

Amara freezes. Closes her eyes and breathes out. *Fine.* It's always the hard way. "We could take him along and let the Gray handle him," she whispers back.

Kazimir turns on his heel and starts running.

"It's not worth the risk," Jesse says, as Kazimir gets farther and farther away. "The planet gave me two more lives, no more and no less, but it doesn't care which ones." A golden curl falls over his eyebrow as he cants his head, considering. "So I'd like to propose an alternative solution."

Amara's shoulders slump in defeat. "Go ahead—"

Jesse moves, quick as lighting. Amara pulls in a panicked breath. Before she has a chance to push it out again, he's caught up to Kazimir and has dragged him back into the shadows. Jesse's hands cradle the man's head, his eyes glowing a little brighter. Kazimir opens his mouth to cry out, but then Jesse's fingers sink through his face as though through clay.

Kazimir gurgles helplessly.

"I'm sorry," Jesse says, pressing his fingers in deeper. "But this is going to hurt."

"No," Kazimir croaks. "No. Please. Toyin."

Jesse shakes his head mournfully, but his lips crack open into a grin. It's a fixed, pained thing, as if the rest of his face disagrees with his mouth. But it's still a smile. "I did say this was unfortunate."

"Toyin," Kazimir says again. "Our daughter. No."

"Don't worry." Jesse's flawless face goes molten, euphoric. "It's fine. Become unmade."

The luminescence of his eyes renders everything in exquisite, blinding, nightmarish detail. Kazimir's flesh sloughs off his skull in steaming, stinking chunks until only gleaming bone remains. His eyes roll back and pour over his dripping cheeks, thick tears of vitreous gel. His once-smiling lips slip off and his jaw unhinges, revealing tender pink gums dissolving into blood and tissue. His liquefied tongue, bubbling and oozing, pours from between pristine white teeth.

This is what will happen to Henry.

Amara expects to feel disgust at or even remorse for his fate, but all she feels is relief. When the Gray is through with the man, he will be well and truly gone. The only person remaining in Vinh's heart will be her.

No one else.

Jesse pries his perfectly clean fingers from the remnants of Kazimir's head. The body crumples to the ground with a wet thump. The skull pops off and rolls into the neatly trimmed grass at the side of the path. It does not occur to Amara that Jesse could've easily snapped Kazimir's neck and been done with it.

"Did I frighten you?" Jesse hasn't turned around yet, but Amara still feels like he's looking right at her. "I'm sorry if I did."

"You don't scare me. Not any more than I do myself." Honesty is deliciously easy when there's no reason to hide. And she has a question of her own: "Will you grieve for them?"

"No. But I'll grieve for the fact that they made me . . . made the planet do this." Jesse sighs. "I'm not sorry this world is ending for humans. Come on."

They meet Vinh at the agreed-upon spot, halfway to the settlement's hangar. Vinh keeps looking back as they prepare the helicraft for takeoff. The third time, Amara reaches out and puts a cool hand on Vinh's shoulder, her fingers brushing the other woman's neck.

"What's wrong?" And because Amara can't help herself,

she adds, "If you forgot something, it'll still be here waiting for us when we return."

She counts precisely four seconds before her wife answers. They're long seconds.

"It's Henry." Vinh crosses her arms over her chest. "I was going to try to bring him along."

"The planet granted me only two lives," says Jesse.

"I know." Vinh gnaws at her bottom lip. "I was hoping we could ask for one more. He loved me, even though I told him I could never reciprocate. He was kind, and we respected each other. I had to try."

"I guess he changed his mind," Amara says softly. Her hands itch to touch her own face, to make sure her expression gives nothing away.

Vinh's eyes bore into hers for a long moment. She stops looking back.

002

They follow Jesse up the crater of the ancient hollow. He stops every twenty meters to let them catch up, waiting patiently while Amara and even Vinh sweat and pant behind him.

"We never figured out why the rock here looks so strange," he says, apropos of nothing, when they catch up. His luminous eyes bore into Amara.

She tries not to fidget as she catches her breath. The honed attention isn't exactly unnerving. It's just that Jesse used to hate making prolonged eye contact, even with loved ones.

"But I suppose we'll have all the time in the world," he continues.

Amara nods. She doesn't really care what they do, so long as they do it together.

They peer over the rim as night dissolves into day. Gray bubbles and froths in the hollow, like liquid pearl inside a gleaming shell. It looks like an ending and a beginning, like rebirth. Like falling in love.

Amara holds a hand out to Vinh, heart thrumming against her ribs. There are no buildings this far out, and so there's no light pollution. She can see the flicking, fading pattern of the stars reflected in Vinh's eyes. Her wife has never looked more beautiful.

"Ready?" Amara asks. *Can you forgive me? Even though you know I'm not sorry. Even though you know I'd do it again.*

"I am." Vinh doesn't hesitate. There is a heavy sort of forbearance in her eyes. Between the constellations in her irises is the acceptance of someone who has no choice but to move forward. She grips Amara's fingers, pulls her in as close as she did on that faraway station years ago. "I love you." She says it severely, in the voice of a field medic assessing a terminal injury.

How can she? How could anyone? How do you return to a dream you know is nothing but a fantasy, once you've lived through a nightmare you've learned to accept?

"I know," says Amara. It hurts like the truth but it tastes like a lie. "I love you too. Is that all right?"

Vinh looks at her. Really looks, like Amara has the answer to every question in the universe. No—she looks at Amara like she *is* the answer. Or perhaps even a universe all on her own. It is unsteadying.

"Yes," says Vinh. And yet, it is not a look of awe or affection. It is a calculating look, the look of a woman realizing the problem that's been plaguing her has but a single, bruisingly simple solution. "Yes. Please."

They step off the edge.

001

The sun rises.

Jesse sits at the edge of the hollow, watching his host star ascend gracefully into the sky. He has been cleansed, at long last. Amara and Vinh are gone, forever. The sacred truth of it is a sweet ache in the bones of his flesh body and in the body below and all around him. He sighs, utterly content as he reclines against living stone. He's given his beloved friends a beautiful tomb.

He is the world and the world is him. He feels the delicate slide of a pale, unseeing worm across the bottom of a cave kilometers away. He feels a dawn-blooming flower unfurl itself to the morning, releasing a puff of sweet perfume at the bottom of the hollow. He feels a six-legged asterfish slither after prey in the ocean on the other side of the planet. He feels an insect soar among the clouds above, its iridescent wings catching the very first rays.

And then . . .

There is a sudden change, and he feels that too.

Vinh—

Amara—

I can see you. I can see everything.

You're . . . We're everything.

Jesse?

Jesse?

It's them. He hears their voices echo deep in his skull, beautiful and unbound. He thought he'd cared for them back then, but what he felt pales to nothingness beside the emotion that takes root within him now. He loves them as no lone human has ever loved before.

I'm here, he says. *Join me,* he adds, partly a joke.

They might not have understood before, but they do now. Of course they do. He tastes the feather-light tickle of their answering amusement.

Amara and Vinh are gone, just as he was.

They're something different now, something new. They are one with the planet. They are one with him, around him and in him and of him. Indivisible, forever. They'll never ignore him again. They will never not see or not think of or not be with him again. They will never not *be* him. They have each other.

They have the Gray. No one and nothing else. That is all they will ever need.

In a way, Jesse has had the Gray for some time now. And the Gray has had him. They were both quiet creatures. They never meant to be bringers of death and destruction. And yet. Jesse goaded Vinh into killing the captives. The planet devoured Jacksonhaven. What further proof could he need? He and the Gray have changed each other for the better. And there is still more change on the horizon.

Jesse doesn't turn around as Amara and Vinh—a wild and gorgeous union of themselves and himself and the Gray—claw their way out of their new womb. For that is what this hollow is, a place of birthing as well as a place of final rest. His chest fills with joy and gratitude, both his and theirs and the planet's. None of them will ever have to be alone again. And there will be no refuge from paradise.

"Come sit by us," they say, "and watch our sunrise."

This world is theirs.

000

In the far reaches of space, a new world observes the life It has remade, and perceiving this new life to be very good, is pleased once more.

ACKNOWLEDGMENTS

On May 17, 2021, I began writing what would one day become the book you're holding now. If I'm being entirely honest, I have no recollection of doing so, and I only know the date because I just went back and checked. But given that this happened during quarantine, that's par for the course. What I do remember is the conversation I had with my editor, Jen Gunnels, and my agent, Tricia Skinner, sometime later, where we discussed turning the original short story into something much longer. They saw the fully realized horror this could be even before I did, and I am so grateful for it.

It's been a dream come true to work with the fantastic team at Nightfire, especially Aislyn Fredsall, Rachel Taylor, Laura Etzkorn, Greg Collins, Esther Kim, Dakota Griffin, Rafal Gibek, Steven Bucsok, Lauren Hougen, Ed Chapman, and Marla Pachter.

Thank you to the fabulous writers and readers who provided early feedback, especially Bill McCane, Haldane B. Doyle, Bill Adler, and Even Han.

Many thanks to all the teachers, researchers, professors, advisors, mentors, and labmates who solidified and supported my love of both writing and science. Thank you to Slug Hugs for their expertise and for being hilarious. H., L.,

A., and E. kindly described the finer details of mountain formation and composition, explained the various reasons for licking rocks (H., I hope you get that park shale out of your mouth), and their reactions to that one scene—you know the one—made me laugh so hard I nearly cried. (A., I am incredibly honored you selected this as your "one [redacted] book" of 2024.) It's a privilege and a joy to get paid to learn, and doubly so to learn from and with the incredible research groups my PIs have built. (Though I hope they haven't read this.)

And, of course, thank you to my family and friends. I owe a particular debt to my big brother Josh—who did not make fun of me when I described the sort of creature this novella was turning into—and to Ivy, Melodey, Lianne, Andrea, and Julia—who *did* make fun of me, but in a way that had my sides splitting all over again. Family friends Dì Hùng and Cậu Hiền and author Thúy Nguyễn kindly checked my Vietnamese. Any errors are my fault alone.

Finally, I would like to thank everyone fighting for equality and for justice; for the inalienable rights under attack; and for the freedom of all people to be whoever they are in peace and to love, or not love, whomever they want. Thank you for working to make the world a better, safer, kinder place.

ABOUT THE AUTHOR

KEMI ASHING-GIWA enjoys learning about the real universe as much as she likes making ones up. She stud-
ied integrative biology and astrophysics at Harvard, and is
now pursuing a Ph.D. in the Earth and Planetary Sciences
department at Stanford. She has published several short stories with *Reactor*, Anathema Publishing, *The Sunday Morning
Transport*, *Clarkesworld Magazine*, and others. *This World Is Not
Yours* is her first novella.